A Highland Fling

Playing for Blood II

By
Chuck Anderson

PublishAmerica
Baltimore

© 2009 by Chuck Anderson.
All rights reserved. No part of this book may be reproduced, stored in a retrieval system or transmitted in any form or by any means without the prior written permission of the publishers, except by a reviewer who may quote brief passages in a review to be printed in a newspaper, magazine or journal.

First printing

All characters in this book are fictitious, and any resemblance to real persons, living or dead, is coincidental.

PublishAmerica has allowed this work to remain exactly as the author intended, verbatim, without editorial input.

ISBN: 1-60813-091-6
PUBLISHED BY PUBLISHAMERICA, LLLP
www.publishamerica.com
Baltimore

Printed in the United States of America

This book is dedicated to Arnold Peterson, who taught me how to wrestle; and to Dr. Harry Garvin, who taught me how to write.

Dear Joe,

A lot has happened since I took your money at the Mid-Ocean Club in Bermuda. Any time you want to play there again, I will be glad to give you a return match—double or nothing this time?

As you may or may not have heard, Mack and I retired from teaching at about the same time, and set up a private detective agency in his garage. We had mostly small jobs at first, investigating disability cheaters and folks who set their cars on fire to get out of expensive leases. We saw ourselves as the Sherlock Holmes and Dr. Watson of the computer age, while the local police saw us as something of a joke, Abbot and Costello as private eyes, maybe Mutt and Jeff.

Anyway, their perception of us changed slightly when we got involved in a murder case. It seems that a Colombian drug cartel was smuggling cocaine into Long Island, using a local football coach and some of his players in their operation. It turns out the Colombians had bigger plans, when we found out they were trying to launder their ill-gotten gains by buying into a golf course/condominium complex.

We didn't really solve the case, according to John Hightower, the local chief. But we kept "stirring the pot," as he put it, until things became so uncomfortable for the coach and his drug overlords that they started making mistakes.

The whole thing came to a head at the U.S. Open in Shinnecock, when one of the kids involved in the drug operation, one of the Gonzago twins—remember those bad apples?—stabbed Mack with a plastic tent peg. Fortunately, his aim was not too good, and Mack was left with an uncomfortable but not fatal wound in his back.

While Mack was recovering, we took a trip to Florida, visiting Key West with Dan and Belle Laybourne—you may remember them. When we got home, the drug mob sent the Gonzago twins to take another run at us, this time out on Great South Bay. We were lucky again, and managed to avoid being swept out to sea at the Shinnecock Inlet, thanks to Juan, Maria's son. Dom Evangelista, the kid who was such a hell-raiser back in high school, became a bounty hunter, and tracked the twins who had tried to kill us to the airport in Miami. He nabbed them just as they were boarding a plane for Colombia. He chained them up in the back of his van and brought them back to New York to stand trial.

Mack and Maria got married last month, and are on their way to Scotland for a honeymoon. Seems he wants to show her where his ancestors came from, the ones who fought in the Battle of Culloden, something like that. I think he wants to play a little golf while he's there. He can use the practice, that's for sure.

Carol and I have separated again. We still care for each other, but she says she "needs some space." Also says she can't stand my cigars, and my current obsession, looking for gold doubloons on the beach with a metal detector. She has taken our grandchildren to stay with our son the surgeon in Pittsburgh.

So that's the news from Southport. Hope all is well with you, and if you're not making par, you are at least having fun trying.

Your friend,

Sal

Chapter 1

From: DNA Research.com
To: Macintosh Thomas

Dear Sir:

    We have evaluated the DNA sample swabs you sent us last month. In your letter you indicated that you had been adopted at birth, and had no idea of your heritage. While your name is Scottish, you claimed you had no actual biological proof of Scottish lineage.

    We are pleased to tell you that after entering your results in our world-wide database, it would appear that you have a relative living in Scotland. Last year he sent us a DNA sample, and it matches up with yours.

    As you may have read in our literature, DNA research

shows that all people, regardless of race or ethnicity, can follow their genetic roots back to a group of common ancestors. Your genetic history has become part of an ancestral library that links you with individuals who share similar genetics.

It would appear that you have a cousin living in Nairn, Scotland. His name is Donald Jamieson. You and he share the same DNA, which originated from Iberia.

You may wish to contact him using the email component provided in your DNA research results.

We hope this information will help you add to your family tree.

Sincerely,

Joshua Stewart, MD

Chapter 2

To: WTC Insurance Company
From: Sal Cascio, Investigator

Dear Sirs:

Several months ago you asked me to investigate a claim by New York City Police Detective Harry Valentine, who was forced to retire on medical disability as a result of his exposure to toxins and particulate matter during his three-month tour of duty at the World Trade Center beginning on September 11, 2001.

Valentine is suffering from a number of ailments common to WTC workers.

The plaintiff contends that the city, his employer, failed to provide adequate protective equipment in the form of respirators and hazardous material coveralls, as well as training and supervision at the work site.

When you contacted me regarding this case, you sent a newspaper clipping showing a photo of Valentine running in a foot race, dressed in a nun's habit and wearing high heels. Evidently he was running in a charity race, hoping to win a ticket to a Hannah Montana concert for his daughter.

I agree that on the surface this does not look like a man who should be on medical disability.

Upon further investigation, I have found that Valentine, who is suffering from pulmonary fibrosis and asthma, entered the race to win a ticket for his daughter because he could not afford to purchase one.

I talked to Valentine, and he said, "I have an illness that is getting worse, bills and a mortgage that I can't pay, medications I can't afford. I wanted to do this for my kid."

Valentine's wife said that after the race, he took to his bed for several days.

In spite of the photographic evidence, I do not believe that Valentine's actions constitute disability fraud.

It seems to me that the WTC Insurance Company has bigger fish to fry than going after a man who is trying to do something for his little girl.

Respectfully,

Sal Cascio

Chapter 3

Email from Scotland

Dear Sal,

Maria and I arrived safely after a trip that took longer than I expected. We had to fly to Manchester, England, then take a flight from there to Glasgow. At Glasgow, we took a train to Inverness. All of this took about three days.

We rented a car in Inverness, and after a day or two of near accidents, we got used to the "roundabouts." I know, I know, you're probably saying, "What is he doing behind the wheel of a car? He hasn't driven in years."

Well, you're right. But I am finding out I still have some of those skills left in the motor part of my brain. (No pun intended.) Nevertheless, Maria has insisted that I turn in the car in Nairn, our first stop. Will write to you when we get there. We will have to rely on public transportation, after all.

Your friend and associate,

Mack

Chapter 4

Email from Mack

Sal: I hope you get this soon. I need your help. Maria and I were walking along the edge of the woods that run along the golf course at Nairn, and she was shot by a guy who claimed he was hunting rabbits. The wound is not life-threatening, but she was shot in the leg and will be laid up for a couple of weeks. Something about this looks fishy, and I could use your help.
Come.

Mack

When I got this email from Mack, I decided to cash in one of the gold doubloons I found on the beach near the

Treasure Oak golf course. I took it down to the local mint. When I walked into that establishment, John Orlando, the proprietor, looked up from a catalogue he was perusing and said, "Sal! Haven't seen you in a while. Have you given any thought to selling any of those doubloons you found?"

I said, "John, you old crook. You know that's why I'm here."

"Now, Sal, you know I will give you a fair price. Thanks to you, my kid graduated from high school."

"Aw, he would have made it anyway. All I did was give him a boot in the ass when he needed it."

Nevertheless, John was overjoyed to take the gold off my hands, at probably a fraction of the price I could have gotten on EBay.

Next problem: I knew my passport was still valid, but I couldn't find it. I called Carol in Pittsburgh.

"Hi, babe. How are you doing?"

"Fine, Sal. And the twins are thriving in the clean air."

"Clean air? Pittsburgh?"

"Yes, since they closed down most of the steel mills, the air has improved a lot. I can't say as much for the economy, but the medical business is still thriving. Your son is busier than ever."

"Well, he should be, as one of the leading thorasic surgeons in the midwest. But that's not why I'm calling. I've got to go to Scotland, and I can't find my passport."

"I had a feeling you wouldn't be able to be separated from Mack for long. Besides, I know you want to play golf over there."

"No, that's not it, really. Some guy who claims he was hunting rabbits near a golf course shot Maria in the leg. Mack sent me an email, asking me to come."

"Oh Sal. That's terrible. On her honeymoon, too. Well, you must go, of course. Mack is helpless in these situations."

"You're right. Now, what about my passport?"

"It's in the safe deposit box in the bank. I put it there with a bunch of other papers before I left. You have the key, right?"

"Yeah, I know where it is. Hanging on the key rack. Thanks, babe. I'll see you when I get back. My love to the kids."

"Oh, and Sal, be careful over there. You don't have the local cops to watch your back the way they do in Southport."

I sent a telegram to Mack, and went down to the local travel agent to get a ticket for Scotland. It turns out I had to take the same convoluted route that led Mack and Maria to that country: British Airways to Manchester, Scotch Air to Glasgow, train to Inverness, and rental car to Nairn.

Just in case, I packed my golf clubs. After all, you never know when the opportunity arises, and I had always wanted to play at the home of the great game.

Chapter 5

"Scotland, a land of meanness, sophistry, and mist."
—George Gordon, Lord Byron

As I sat in the train that wound its way through the highlands to Nairn, I looked up the town of Nairn in the guidebook, and read: "the Nairn Golf Course, one of the oldest in Scotland, is bordered on one side by Birnam Wood. From every hole, one may see the Firth of Moray. In the late 1800's the course was extended westward over the Earl of Cawdor's property."

I mused over the words: "Birnam Wood, Moray, Cawdor." Now it is the curse of every English teacher worth his salt, retired or not, to respond to certain words and ideas that he has tried to pound into the heads of reluctant scholars. Memories of Macbeth floated through my mind as the rhythmic clicking of the old railroad almost put me to sleep.

Mack and I had often played a game called Identify the Quote, especially when waiting to tee off in a slow round of golf. Lines like, "Strike, brave boys, and take your turn," "Your play needs no excuse," and "What subtle hole is this?" Shakespeare seemed to provide a quote for every situation, and many sports.

The Bard was born roughly a hundred years after the game of golf was played at Bruntsfield Links in Edinburgh, and according to the history of the game, it was firmly established by the time he was writing a play about Macbeth, the Thane of Moray and Cawdor.

Shakespeare wrote the final version of the *Tragedie of Macbeth* in 1606, when stories of witches, prophesy, treason, murder, and execution were topics that fascinated King James VI of Scotland (James I of England) to the point of obsession.

The guide book noted that Cawdor Castle, still standing, was built in the late 14th century near Birnam Wood and the Firth of Moray.

As the train pulled into the Inverness Station, my reveries ended, and I began to think about the real world and the problem of Mack and Maria.

After the scenic grandeur of the trip across the

Highlands, Inverness was a bit of a let down. The city was on a flat plain, divided by the River Ness, that wound through the center of town beside high-spired churches.

The guide book pointed out that the best sights in Inverness were not within the city limits. Just five miles out of town was the Culloden Battlefield, with its clan graves, Well of the Dead, Memorial Cairn, and Old Leanach Farmhouse, the site of Bonnie Prince Charlie's fiasco in 1746 and the last land battle on British soil.

Thirteen miles northeast of Inverness is Cawdor Castle, where, according to Shakespeare, Macbeth stabbed King Duncan. The castle has everything: a drawbridge, a tower built around a tree, a freshwater well inside the house, a maze, gardens, nature trails, a pitch and putt golf course, and a gift shop.

Across the street from the train station in Inverness, I found an Avis rental agency, and booked a car. As I filled out the paperwork, the agent reminded me that driving in England was not like the States. "Remember," he said, "in Britain, we drive on the opposite side of the road. Also, the steering wheel is on the right side of the car."

Then, to add to my nervousness, he said, "And mind the roundabouts."

I quickly learned about the British addition to the civilized driving world, as there did not seem to be any intersections with stoplights. As I entered my first round about, I automatically looked the wrong way, expecting traffic to be headed from the right. Fortunately, I looked the other way at the last minute, just avoiding a collision with a lorry.

I finally got on the A96, also known as the Old Military Road, to Nairn.

Chapter 6

"Oh, you take the high road and I'll take the low road, and I'll be in Scotland afore ye."
—Anon.

On the way into Nairn, I passed an open field that looked like a campground, filled with trailers. There was a sign that read, "New Age Travelers Caravan Park," but I didn't think much about it at the time. Later, I would find that New Age Travelers were, in fact, modern Gypsies, sometimes disparagingly called "dole moles," itinerant folk who would show up at a post office, collect their monthly dole check, and move on. They didn't like to be called "gypsies," either, but referred to themselves as "The Romani."

Arriving in town, I stopped and got directions at an information center to the Firthside Hotel, where Mack was supposed to be staying.

As I walked through the small lobby of the hotel, I saw several sets of golf clubs stacked in a corner, along with jackets, hats, and rain gear, all set aside for the convenience of the guests. I went to the front desk and a rang the bell. Shortly, a young man with red hair came out of a back room, wiping his hands on a towel, saying, "Yes? May I help you, sir?"

"Yes, I'm just in from America, and I am looking for a friend of mine who is staying here. His name is Macintosh Thomas."

"Ah, yes, the unfortunate Mr. Thomas. He is not here at present."

"Why do you say 'unfortunate'? And where is he at present?"

"Sorry, sir, we are all most distressed at the unfortunate accident that injured the lovely Mrs. Thomas. I believe you will find Mr. Thomas at her bedside in the hospital."

"And where might I find the hospital?"

"You will have to head back to the center of town, find High Street, turn left. High Street will become Cawdor Street, which in turn, becomes Cawdor Road. Just after the football playing fields, you will see the hospital on your right."

I thanked the young man and assumed he went back to the haggis or whatever Scottish delicacy he was consuming for lunch. His directions turned out to be pretty decent, for in about twenty minutes I was pulling into the hospital parking lot.

Chapter 7

I was given a visitor's pass to Maria's room and found it at the end of a long hallway that ran down one of the wings of the hospital. Maria was lying in a bed, pale but alert. She looked up as I entered, and smiled, saying, "Mack, look who is here. It's Sal."

Mack had been standing at the window, telephone in hand, absorbed in a conversation. He turned, and a broad smile lit up his features.

"Hey, buddy, you didn't waste any time getting here. I didn't expect you until tomorrow."

"Oh, you know me. When duty calls, and all that."

"Yeah, well, I'm really glad you're here, pal."

"Me, too," Maria said faintly. I turned to look at her, and she looked very tired and vulnerable.

Mack said, "They got the pellets out all right, but a

secondary infection has developed in the wound. They're treating it with antibiotics, but she's still a little weak."

I said, "Let's go get a cup of coffee and let her rest."

Mack answered, "Good idea. Maria, you take it easy for awhile, sweetie. We'll be right back."

Maria smiled wanly, glad to see me, but glad for a litte peace and quiet, evidently.

We went downstairs to the coffee shop, which had the appearance of an old-fashioned tea room.

Fortunately, they had good strong coffee in addition to various selections of tea, such as Earl Gray. I picked up a couple of scones with a pot of jam to go with my coffee, and we sat down at a window table overlooking a spacious lawn at the back of the hospital.

Mack said, "Well, we've been gone for a short time, but we have a lot of catching up to do. First, how did you like the trip over?"

"Man, I wouldn't want to do that again. The trip took me seven hours plus. I could have flown to Sicily in the same time, and the food is better down there."

"You're right about that. Anyway, let me tell you what happened."

"Yeah, that's why I'm here. Though I did bring my clubs along, just in case."

"You never give up, do you? Well, Maria and I were taking a walk along the Nairn golf course, the one that runs along the

Firth of Moray. It was after dinner, but it stays light so late around here, it was like late afternoon. We were walking along the third hole, along the edge of the rough. And believe me, the course has a lot of rough. They call it 'gorse' over here."

"So how did Maria get shot?"

"She saw some flowers at the edge of the woods, and followed a kind of path into the undergrowth. I yelled at her to wait for me, then there was a shot. When I caught up with her, Maria was on the ground, holding her leg. She told me to give her my belt, to make a tourniquet, as cool as a cucumber. Must have been her medical training taking over."

"Who shot her?"

"I was getting to that. Just then this jocko came out of the woods, holding a gun under his arm. He called out, 'I say, are you all right there?' I was about to slug the guy, but Maria said, 'Mack, you have to get me out of here.' Seeing Maria on the ground, the guy was all apologies, saying he had taken a shot at a rabbit and missed. He had a cell phone, and called what passes for emergency services over here. An ambulance arrived in about ten minutes, and took Maria and me here to the hospital."

"What was the shooter's name?"

"He introduced himself, like he was at a tea party. His name was Harry Soames."

I said, "You stay here with Maria. I think I'm going to have a talk with Mr. Soames."

Chapter 8

Returning to the hotel, I asked my friend the desk clerk for a local phone directory. There was a "Harry Soames" listed as living at 25 Gordon Street. The clerk rang him up, and handed me the telephone.

"Mr. Soames? My name is Salvatore Cascio, and I represent Mrs. Thomas, who was involved in an unfortunate shooting accident. I would like to speak with you about it, clear up the details for the insurance, you know."

The next day, I knocked on the door of 25 Gordon Street, a pleasant brick cottage with a front yard ablaze with roses. Many of the houses on the street had similar collections of vivid roses, thanks to the Gulf Stream and the temperate climate. A middle-aged gentleman answered. The middle-aged paunch, balding head with a comb-over, rimless glasses—he looked like a retired bank clerk, not someone who would be going around shooting tourists from America.

"Yes? Are you Cascio?"

"Yes, I called you yesterday."

I presented one of my business cards, which lists me as an insurance investigator, among other things. He peered at the card through bifocal glasses, then said,

"Won't you come in?"

As we settled in his comfortable living room over cups of tea served by his wife, Soames said, "I do hope there isn't going to be a lawsuit or something like that. I am retired, and we have very little in the way of assets."

His wife stood by the doorway, wringing her hands on a dishtowel.

"No, no. It's nothing like that," I said. "I'm just here to gather information on behalf of the Thomas couple. Their insurance will take care of the medical bills, and they are not the kind of people who sue at the drop of a hat."

Soames said, "I feel terrible about the whole thing."

Suddenly Mrs. Soames spoke up. "Harry, tell the man. Tell him what happened to our Mary. Maybe he will understand."

Soames flushed bright red, and turned to his wife angrily. "These people don't know about us, about Mary."

His wife said, "Tell him, Harry. Maybe he will understand."

Harry started slowly, reluctantly, embarrassed by what he perceived as a personal failure, "We have one child, a daughter Mary. We were very proud of her. She went off to university in Glasgow, and when she returned for Christmas break, she was somehow changed."

Mrs. Soames said, "I was cleaning her room one day, and found some strange medical paraphernalia."

Soames broke in bitterly, "Mary picked up some bad habits while away at school. Soon she would go off in the evenings, and return late at night."

Mrs. Soames said, "We never knew where she went or what she was doing, but she seemed listless, shut off to us."

"One evening," Harry said, "I decided to follow her to find out where she went. I tracked her to a seaside carnival, down near the Promenade. There were rides and games of chance. I saw her enter the tent of a gypsy fortune teller. A few minutes later, she came out of the tent with a swarthy woman, and they walked down the fairway towards a collection of wagons."

At this point in his narration, Soames became very agitated. He stammered, "I didn't mean to take a shot at your friend's wife. I don't know what came over me. I was hunting rabbits. But when I saw this woman with the same dark hair and swarthy skin coming towards me, something snapped. I thought it was the gypsy who had corrupted my daughter. I saw red, and shot. I'm really sorry. I didn't mean to hurt her. I just wanted to scare the gypsy the way she has scared me."

I said, "Thank you for being so forthcoming. I'm sure Mr. and Mrs. Thomas have no intention of pressing charges. They see the whole thing as an accident, and are not the kind of people to be vindictive. But I am concerned about your daughter. Where is she now?"

Mrs. Soames spoke up, "We haven't seen her since she went off with that awful woman. We don't know what to do. We don't want to call the police. It would hurt her chances at the university if she were arrested."

I said, "I think her safety is the most important thing here, don't you?"

Soames looked at the floor, and his wife continued wringing the towel in her hands.

"Look," I said, "I'm going to be in town for a week or so while my friends get squared away. Maybe I'll go down to that carnival and look around. Do you have a photograph of your daughter I could borrow?"

They were so grateful, you would think I was a knight in shining armor, well, a Sicilian knight in tarnished armor, but you get the picture. Besides, I kind of felt sorry for the couple, who were clearly not in touch with the modern world.

Chapter 9

"Scotland, a land of brown heath and shaggy wool, land of the mountains and the flood."
—Sir Walter Scott

I went down to the seaside carnival, only to find that the fortune teller was no longer there. In fact, it looked like the whole carnival was packing up to move on. There was a lone zeppoli vendor in a forlorn truck in the corner of the lot. I decided to try some Scottish zeppoli, which sounds like an oxymoron or at the least an anachronism. It was neither, just bad fried dough, but the proprietor gave me some information. He said, "Most of the folks in this carnival are gypsies, lad. They move from resort to resort. I think they're headed to an encampment over near Culloden, for the battle re-enactment next week." I remembered the gypsy camp I had seen on my way into town, and wondered if if was the same bunch. I decided to have another zeppoli, for one is never enough. This seemed to encourage the vendor, who continued his commentary on the gypsies.

"Like every group, there's good 'uns and bad 'uns. Some are respectable, god-fearing folk. The government had to pass some laws a while back, keeping folks from persecuting them."

I said, "Nothing new there. When Hitler was trying to purify the Aryan bloodline, the gypsies were among the first to be sent to the gas chambers."

"And of course there's all those old stories, about gypsies kidnapping children, stealing and the like."

"That's not unusual. They said the same thing about my ancestors in Sicily."

Chapter 10

I decided to check in with Mack and Maria to tell them what I had found out.

Returning to the hospital, I found Mack packing up Maria's things. "Where's Maria?" I asked.

Mack said, "She's with the doctor. The wound is healing, but too slowly for his comfort. And mine. He has recommended a stay at a kind of spa near here, a place called the 'Findhorn' foundation.' They send patients there from this hospital. I guess it's a good place to rest and rehabilitate."

I told Mack what I had found out about the shooting. He said, "The poor guy. Sounds like he's got more problems than he can handle. That's no excuse to take a pot shot at American tourists, though. It's bad for business."

I said, "What do you think we should do about Mr. Soames?"

Mack answered, "Right now, my first concern is Maria. Let's get her over to this rehab place the doctor has recommended. Look it over. If she's comfortable there, maybe we can look into this other thing while we're waiting for her to recover. I wish we could get her back to the states, though. But the doctor said extensive travel might not be good for her."

I said, "Well, the United States is supposed to have the best medical care in the world, but I read someplace that Scotland ranks higher. Haggis and health care…go figure."

Chapter 11

The next day, we took a cab to the Findhorn place. As we followed a winding road up to the community, we saw some strange-looking buildings, which looked like inverted whiskey barrels. Surrounding the complex were extensive gardens, tended by young people who looked as if they enjoyed working with the land. They weren't exactly singing, but they looked healthy and somehow exuberant, as if they enjoyed being there.

"I hope you don't expect me to stay in one of those," said Maria.

The cab driver spoke up, "Actually, M'am, those are recycled whiskey vats from the local distillery. They're supposed to be quite comfy."

Mack said, "No, the rehab place is in the main building. It has hot tubs, a massage and therapy center. We'll check it out."

Later, after finding the facilities acceptable, we located Maria in a private room with a nice view of the garden. She looked at us, standing around with our hands in our pockets, and said, "You two look out of place here. Why don't you go play a round of golf?"

I said, "Are you sure? Are you comfortable here?"

"Yes," Maria said, "and I have a good book to read. Mack gave it to me. It's called *Mary, Queen of Scots*, by Antonia Frazer. Did you know that Queen Mary played golf?"

Mack said, "Yeah, and I bet nobody questioned her about her handicap. If they had, she would have had their heads cut off."

He added, "Are you sure you are going to be O.K., darlin'?"

Maria said, "Yes, yes. I would rather be alone with a good book than try to entertain you two sad sacks. Now, get out of here."

Chapter 12

That afternoon, Mack and Sal found themselves on the historic course at Nairn. As they struggled to keep their drives out of the gorse, two figures watched from the edge of the woods. One was swarthy, with long, flowing black hair, a mustache, and a gold earring. He was known locally as Joseph Caddy, said to be the head of a gypsy clan that lived near Nairn. In another country, at another time, he was called Kaffir Selin, member of a Turkish terrorist group, but few people knew that.

With him was a man with no country, a man named Leroy Kemp. Kemp was a large, florid man with wide shoulders and meaty hands. In his day, he had been a devastating defensive tackle, and had left a trail of broken noses in his wake. His nose had also taken a beating in the football wars, and excessive drink had left a spray of broken capillaries across the expansive area between his eyes.

As they watched the golfers, Kemp said, "I have a score to settle with those two clowns. They cost me a wife, my standing in the community, my pension. I can't go back to the states, thanks to their bumbling interference."

"Why not, my friend?"

"There's a warrant out for my arrest. It's a good thing our friends in Colombia have set me up here as an exporter of Scotch whiskey."

"And as as importer of cocaine," said his bewhiskered associate.

Chapter 13

> "Scots who have with Wallace bled,
> Scots, whom Bruce has often led,
> Welcome to your gory bed
> Or to victory."
> —Robert Burns

As we played the old course at Nairn, I had the uncanny feeling that we were being watched. Losing a couple of golf balls to the gorse on each hole was bad enough, but having someone observe our inept attempts at making par at least one hole was downright embarrassing. At one point, Mack said, "See those two guys up on the hill?"

"Where?" I said as I drove another ball into the Firth of Moray.

"Up on that hill over there," he said.

I looked, but didn't see anybody. "I don't see anyone."

"They probably backed into the trees," Mack said. "They must be watching us for a reason."

I thought: "Why would a couple of bird watchers be interested in American golfers?" We certainly weren't playing well enough to warrant any local interest.

As we left the course during the purple shadows of what they call over in Scotland "the gloaming," that time of day when the country seems to settle into itself, I said to Mack, "Say, did you give any more thought to that DNA relative of yours?"

"Oh, you mean Donald Jamieson? No. I was so preoccupied with Maria, it left my mind."

"Why don't we look him up in the phone book before we go back to Findhorn? We have to go through town to get there."

We went to the information center in town, and Mack looked up the name of his remote "cousin" in the telephone directory. He found a number for Jamieson and dialed it. The man's wife answered, and told Mack her husband was at work.

Mack said, "He's at work here in town. Why don't we stop by and pay him a visit?"

"Where does he work?" I asked.

"Interestingly enough," Mack said, "we can find him at

the local police station. Would you believe, he's a cop. A detective inspector, to be exact."

"Wow, maybe he can help us out," I said.

"Yeah, unless he, like many of our friends in law enforcement, doesn't like amateur detectives, especially American amateur detectives," Mack said.

"You may be right," I said, "why don't we go there and you can introduce yourself with the DNA thing? You sent him an e-mail, right?"

"That's a good idea. Let's see what he's like, besides the genetics," Mack answered.

Chapter 14

We found the police station in Nairn easily enough, as it was not far from the information center. We entered the station, and found a female police officer sitting behind a desk. There's something about a woman in a police uniform that really does it for me, especially if she's directing traffic. Must be something Freudian, but I sure like the sight of a woman in uniform, especially a young one, as this one was. She stood up as we entered: crisp white shirt with epaulets, gray skirt, legs that seemed to go on forever.

"Yes, may I help you gentlemen?"

Mack spoke up, "We're here to see Detective Inspector Jamieson. Is he in?"

"Yes, I believe he is. I'll ring him up. Who shall I say is here to see him?"

"Macintosh Thomas, from the States. I believe he will recognize the name."

She dialed a number on the phone, and shortly, a booming voice was heard echoing down the hall. An inner door swung open, and a giant of a man barged through. He must have been close to seven feet, with sparkling blue eyes and a handle bar mustache.

"Maggie, here's that genetic cousin from the states I was telling you about," he said with a laugh.

His handshake was the proverbial grip of steel, and I consider myself pretty strong after all those years of coaching wrestling.

He sized Mack up, and said, "Well, you're tall, and we have the same color hair. But I've got a few pounds on you, mate."

He turned to me, and said, "Who's your shorter friend?"

As Mack introduced me, I found it hard to take umbrage with this jovial giant's remarks.

He said, "It's almost lunch time. Let's go around the corner to the pub and have a pint. It's a better place to get acquainted."

After two or three pints and a quick overview of their respective family histories, we told Inspector Detective Jamieson about Maria's shooting and my subsequent investigation of the shooter.

The detective inspector said, "Soames, eh? He's thought

to be a good man. Well respected in the village. Had to retire from the postal service to take care of his wife. Suffering from dementia, poor thing. Can't leave her alone too long. Didn't realize they were having trouble with Mary. Lovely young thing, bright as a penny."

I told him I had done some investigating on my own. "I hope you don't mind," I said. "Our license is only valid in New York State."

Jamieson laughed, and said, "We have a long history of amateur sleuths in Great Britain. Don't forget Miss Marple. You'll be all right as long as you don't break any laws. I would appreciate it if you kept us informed of any developments, however."

Mack and I assured him that we would.

As almost an afterthought, Jamieson said, "I wish I could help you with Mary, but we've had our hands full lately, and we are understaffed."

Mack said, "What's the problem?"

Jamieson said, "First, we have had a continuing problem with the gypsies. They are protected under Scottish law, but they continue to take advantage of the policy. They camp out on national trust land, collect the dole, and lately, we've begun to suspect that they are the root of our latest drug scourge, one that affects many of our young people. Like Mary Soames, it seems."

I said, "So anything we find out might be helpful to you."

"Yes," he said, "and the drug problem has a more insidious companion, prostitution. Many of our young people are turning to prostitution to support their habit."

Mack said, "We have a similar problem in the states, and I read recently that in Spain, a definite connection between gypsies, drugs, and teenage prostitution has been established."

I said, "You said you have another problem you're working on."

"Yes," Jamieson said, "this is more of a global issue, and we are supporting national law enforcement on this one. It seems there has been a rash of accidents on our oil platforms in the North Sea. Some people are thinking sabotage. Aberdeen is the oil capital of northern Europe, you know. They have asked for all law enforcement agencies to look for unusual activity in this area."

Mack's honeymoon (and my golf vacation) in Scotland was beginning to take on a whole new dimension.

We bid farewell to Jamieson after promising to keep in touch. On the way back to Findhorn, Mack said, "I think we need to do some homework on the local situation. I want to find out more about these gypsies, and we need to find out about the oil business in Scotland."

Chapter 15

When we got back to Findhorn, it was early evening, though it didn't seem like it at this northern latitude. Mack said, "I've got to spend some time with Maria. She is probably wondering why it took us so long to play a round of golf. Why don't you go to the computer center and see what you can find out about the Scottish oil industry."

I looked up the oil industry in Scotland on *Wikipedia*. I was surprised to learn that the Scottish waters of the North Atlantic and the North Sea contain the largest oil resources in the European Union, and Scotland is the Union's largest petroleum producer, with the discovery of North Sea oil transforming the Scottish economy. Oil was discovered in the North Sea in 1966, with the first year of full production taking place in 1976. The city of Aberdeen is the center of the oil industry, with the port and harbor serving many of the oil fields off shore. The industry employs 100,000 workers, about six percent of the working population of Scotland. It is estimated that there are reserves of two billion tons of oil in the North Sea, as much as has been produced in the last 25 years.

I thought: "It looks as if there's a lot of money around Aberdeen, a fertile ground for drug abuse. And there seemed to be more to the Scottish economy than whiskey, plaid, and golf."

While I was on the internet, I found another item of interest. It seems that an American billionaire, Laird Gump, was planning to build a $2 billion golf resort near Aberdeen. His plan was being blocked by a fisherman who refused to sell his family farm. The farmer, one Ian McLean, told the ugly American to "take his money and shove it," winning admiration from his neighbors who consider him a local hero. Gump, who is used to getting his way, evidently has declared war on the 55-year-old fisherman. He flew in his private jet to Scotland to examine the farm in question, and called it "disgusting," pointing out the fleet of rusting tractors and oil cans littering the 23-acre farm. Gump, whose father came from Scotland, has offered the farmer $900,000 for the land, which sits right in the middle of his 18-hole-golf course development. "It will never be sold to someone like Laird Gump. Not in my lifetime," the farmer told the local newspaper. "My grandfather fished here, my father fished here, and my uncles fished here," he said, standing by his weathered farmhouse. "I'm not going anywhere."

Chapter 16

"Something wicked this way comes."
Macbeth, Act IV, Sc. 1

On the way back to Findhorn, I stopped at a lovely seaside beach and pavilion for a snack. All that brain work on the internet had made me hungry for some fish and chips with a little vinegar on the side. I took my food to the pavilion, where three old ladies sat in the corner, knitting. I greeted them, and attacked my food.

One of them said, "Ah, but he's a hungry laddie, ain't he?"

The other two just cackled over their knitting. I finished my snack, and was about to leave, when the woman who had spoken said, "I'll bet you're an American, aren't you?"

I said, "Yes, I am. Is it that obvious? Maybe I should have worn my kilt."

"Ah," she said, "you couldn't stand the draft, laddie."

I laughed, and said, "You're probably right."

We chatted a bit, mostly about the difference in the weather between the states and Scotland. The old lady's name was Bella Calder, and her two sisters were called Inez and Margaret, respectively. Bella was a little hard of hearing. It seemed that as a young girl she fell under the ice in a nearby river, and by the time they pulled her out, she was permanently deaf in one ear. I learned this because I had to shout, even on her good side.

As I was about to take my leave, Bella pulled me aside and said, "You seem like a nice lad, Sal. Let me warn you about something."

"What's that?" I said.

Bella looked around, as if there were someone watching, then said, "Beware the Birnam Wood."

"What?" I said, a shiver working its way down my spine.

"That's all I've got to say. Beware the wood, that's all."

Chapter 17

When I got back to Findhorn, Mack and Marie had a surprise for me.

"Guess what, Sal?" said Maria with a smile.

"What?"

"Juan is coming to Scotland!" Juan was Maria's son, a fine young man who, as a boy, had survived the twin hells of El Salvador and the Arizona desert on his way to a new home in America. After finishing high school in Southport, he went on to the local community college, and enrolled in the police science program there. After two years, he passed the New York City Police Academy entrance exam with flying colors, and upon graduation, was assigned to the Community Police Unit in East New York, walking a neighborhood beat. He was fluent in Spanish, of course, and the *abuelitas* loved him, as did most of the shop owners.

Maria said, "He has been given leave to come and see me, isn't that wonderful?"

Mack added, "He's flying in to Aberdeen the day after tomorrow, be there in the morning. Do you think you could go over there and meet him? You still have the rental car, right?"

The next evening, I found myself walking down by the harbor in Aberdeen as the night mist crawled around the docks and cranes, reminding me of Carl Sandburg's poem "Fog." The streetlights cast islands of illumination from one corner to the next. At one corner, a young girl stepped out of the darkness, saying in a low voice, "Want to party, mister?"

She had long black hair and lustrous eyes and looked so innocent, her invitation took me by surprise. I would have been tempted if I were so inclined. It had been a long time after my separation from my wife. However, I had always had an abhorrence of prostitutes, especially young ones. Even in college, when the rest of my fraternity brothers drove up to Williamsport, Pennsylvania, for a night of debauchery, I would go along for the sauna and the masseuse to ease my aching muscles after a particularly strenuous practice, but that was it.

I smiled at the girl and said, "No, thank you, my dear."

The girl shrugged her shoulders, and said, sadly, "Oh, that's all right, mister."

Suddenly she was joined by an older woman, dressed in a

black shawl and long skirt. The girl said to her, "I told you, Magda, I'm no good at this sort of thing."

They disappeared into the mist, the young girl's rear twitching like a cat in heat. She may not have thought she was good at this "sort of thing," but I was sure she had a future in it.

Later, in my hotel room, I had a sudden thought. I took out the photograph that Harry Soames had given me, and sure enough, the girl in the mist looked like his daughter.

Chapter 18

My evening encounter on the docks of Aberdeen was forgotten in the excitement of meeting Juan at the airport the next day. While Juan may be Maria's son, Mack and I have a special feeling in our hearts for this young man, a person who has seen and accomplished so much in a brief lifetime. Short, muscular, clear of eye and purpose, we look upon him as a son of our own. The fact that he saved our lives before we were swept out to sea has only strengthened our feelings. He reminds me of a young Sicilian, fresh off the boat at that age, though I like to think I was better looking.

We met at the arrival gate and embraced.

"Woof!" I said, "I see you've added some muscle."

"Yes, Sal. The physical training at the academy was very demanding. I enjoyed the exercises very much."

"And how is the job going, my young friend. I see they have you in a pretty dangerous neighborhood."

"Oh, the community police work is not that bad, especially in the daytime. Everybody seems to appreciate having a police officer in the neighborhood. The bad people come out at night, and when I have night duty, I have learned to stand my post with a wall at my back, just out of the street light, if there is one still working."

"So, has anyone taken a shot at you?" I knew that clean-cut kids from the suburbs were engaged in a virtual war with the gangs in the city, a kind of culture clash, as it were.

Juan said, "One night, when I first began, the sector car came roaring up to me. The captain leaned out and said, 'Get in, get in!' Just as I got in the back seat of the car, I heard a pinging sound in the metal of the side door. When we got back to the station, we found that someone had peppered the car with an Uzi."

"That's pretty scary. Don't tell your mother about that one, OK?"

"No, Sal, things have been pretty good on the daytime shift, which I get more often than not because of my ability to speak the language."

As I began to fill Juan in about our situation here in Scotland, I had a sudden thought. I said,"I think we will give you a new name over here."

"What do you mean?"

"Well, nobody's called 'Juan' in Scotland. From now on, we will call you 'Ian.'"

Chapter 19

"The best laid plans of mice and men gang aft agley."
—Robert Burns

A week later, Mack and I were playing on a course near Aberdeen. Juan, a.k.a. Ian was caddying, as golf carts were not allowed on this course. We were teeing up on the fifth hole, when another caddy came running up, saying, "Hold on there, would you? The party behind you would like to play through."

Now I realize we were playing slowly, losing balls, digging our way out of crater-sized bunkers, and so forth, but I thought we were moving along at a steady pace. Moreover, it is one of the unwritten rules of golf that the party playing ahead, realizing they may be holding up play, should be the ones to invite the next group to play through. One just does not ask the group ahead if it is all right to play through.

This request put us off a little bit, but Mack said, "Hey, it's all right. Let's take a break and let these guys play through. Maybe it's a local custom we don't know about."

So we sat down on a bench and watched the golfers behind us approach the tee.

One of them, a big guy with flowing blond locks, wearing plaid knickers, strode up to where we were sitting and stuck his hand out. "Thanks so much, chaps. Nice of you to let us play through. Name's Gump, Laird Gump," he said in a booming voice.

Mack stood up, took the proferred hand, and said,"Nice to meet you, Gump. I hear you're building a course of your own in this area."

Gump said, "Yes, we're planning a championship course. We're trying, but this damn fisherman is giving us a hard time. I think he's blocking me to make the price of his farm go up."

Mack said, "Well, I'm sure you'll get your way, Mr. Gump."

Gump smiled like a shark, saying, "Yes, I usually do. Well, thanks again for letting us play through."

With that, he addressed his ball and took a mighty swing, grunting with the effort.

The ball dribbled about thirty feet down the fairway. Juan said, "Looks like it is going to be a long afternoon."

Following the inept foursome down the fairway, Mack went into one of his philosophical rants about golf as a metaphor for life. It was his way of calming me down, and so silly that it usually worked.

"You know, Sal," he said, "the way a person plays golf tells us a lot about him."

"What do you mean, 'The Psychology of Golf?'"

"Well, think about it. You're playing with someone for the first time. On every other hole, he asks for or demands a mulligan when he messes up his drive, or if he hits a drive that is remotely playable, he asks for or demands a 'do-over,' the same as a mulligan. Or when you're about to drive, he starts whistling, playing with his keys, or messing around with his clubs."

"Yeah, that would drive me crazy. Some people might call that 'gamesmanship,' but I would call it cheating."

Mack laughed, then said, "Or what about the guy who kicks his ball from the rough to the fairway and a better lie, or improves the position of the ball, claiming winter rules?"

I said, "That's the kind of guy who forces you to keep track of his score as well as your own, especially if you're playing for money."

"Losing money aside," Mack said, "what does all of this tell you about the guy?"

"It tells me that I don't want to play golf with him again. I played with a guy like this once, his name was Brad

Something. He tried all that stuff, even hit my ball once because it had a better lie. I wanted to punch him out, but golf is supposed to be a gentleman's game."

Mack laughed, then said, "And if you punched him, you can be sure you would be hit with a lawsuit the next day. Guys like this give golf a bad name, that's for sure. But the point I was making is that guys who cheat at golf are probably more likely to be dishonest in all other aspects of their lives, from income tax to marriage."

"That's probably true. By the way, do you know where the word 'mulligan' came from?"

Mack said, "I heard it was the name of a real guy, Buddy Mulligan, who was well-known for playing poor shots at a country club in New Jersey. Another theory is that 'mulligan' is a common Irish name, and is is tied into a time when Irish-Americans were joining fancy golf clubs and were looked down upon as incompetent golfers."

"Well," I said, "I heard another story. The word comes from saloons that, back in the good old days, would place a free bottle of booze on the bar for customers to dip into. The bottle was called a Mulligan, a freebie."

"That's a good one. Now, I've got another one for you. Did you ever hear of a 'gotcha'?"

"No, Professor, but I am sure you will tell me about it."

"Well, three guys who thought they were pretty good golfers were asked by the starter if an old man could make up a foursome. The golfers agreed, as the old guy looked as if he was not much competition. They pointed out to the old guy that they were playing for money, and asked him if that was all right.

The old guy said, "That's all right with me, as long as you give me one 'gotcha' per hole."

The three young golfers agreed, thinking the old guy was thinking of something like a mulligan. The first one got up, addressed his ball, and just as he was about to swing, the old man goosed him with one of his clubs, saying, "Gotcha!"

Mack laughed, and said, "Maybe our friend up ahead needs a Gotcha."

Chapter 20

When we got back to Findhorn, Maria had an announcement. The doctor informed her that she was well enough to travel as long as she favored her bad leg. "That means a wheel chair," Mack said.

"It also means preferred seating on the plane," I added, "I remember a disability case we had, about the guy who got a wheel chair whenever he flew from Long Island to Florida. They were first on, first off the plane every time. Did the same with AMTRAK one year, as I recall, where they get a luxury suite on the ground level of the train."

Juan spoke up, "I'm glad you're feeling better, Mama. I have one more week of leave, and I will go with you."

Mack said, "I will be going, too. It's our honeymoon, after all."

Maria smiled, and said, "No, Mack, you are an excellent

teacher and a sometimes brilliant private investigator, but you are the worst nurse in the world. If you went home with me you would be hovering over me every hour of the day, and at the same time, worrying about Sal and the case he seems to be working on. Besides, Juan and I have traveled long distances before, and this one will be much more comfortable."

Mack didn't look too happy about Maria's plan, but we both knew the woman had a will forged in steel.

She said, "You and Sal should stay here for a few more weeks. Maybe you can help Sal with the Soames case, maybe get in a few more rounds of golf."

So plans were made: during their final week, Mack promised to show Maria around Scotland. He said, "I would like to show you Cawdor Castle, the Battlefield at Culloden, have a picnic on the beach at Nairn, go to the Pringle factory where they make kilts—tourist things. Sal and Juan can work on Sal's case. After all, Juan is the only professional law enforcement officer in the family."

He added, "Besides, Sal can afford to stay a couple of extra weeks doing pro bono work. He may have to dip into his hoard of gold doubloons, however."

At breakfast the next day, Juan told me he would like to attend the annual Findhorn Music Fair. "I saw a show about it on television, '60 Minutes,' I think. It looked pretty exciting, with Romani music, Flamenco dancing. This year they are featuring 'Fanfare Ciocarlia,' a Romani brass band. The music is said to be very soulful."

Mack spoke up from behind a week-late *New York Times*, "In Britain they're called 'buskers,' folks who travel from one place to another, performing music, acrobatics, animal tricks, fire eating, and so forth for tips and gratuities. A lot of pickpockets attend these fairs, too, so watch your wallet."

Juan was right about the Romani music. It was soulful and exciting at the same time. Folks were literally dancing in the aisles. During an intermission, we left the super-heated tent and walked down the fairway, cooling off and looking at the games of skill and chance found in fairs all over the world. I saw my friend with the zeppoli stand and went over to talk and have a bite to eat.

When I returned to Juan, there was a young girl at his side, talking and smiling. I looked more closely. It was Mary Soames. I had told him about her, but had not mentioned her name or showed him her picture. He had managed to strike up a conversation with the girl I was looking for.

Juan said, "Mary, this is my 'Uncle Sal,' from the states."

I'll give it to the girl, she didn't bat a pretty eyelash as she held out her hand. Suddenly she looked over my shoulder, paled, and gripped my hand harder. I turned and saw a couple striding towards us, pushing fairgoers out of the way.

I knew the woman. She was the gypsy who went off with Mary that night in Aberdeen.

At the woman's side was a tall, muscular man, with long black hair in a pony tail, a sweeping mustache, and a gold ring in his ear.

They came closer. Just then a huge hand clapped me on the shoulder and a familiar voice boomed out, "Why, here's my friend from the states, the shorter one. Sal Cascio, right? And where's my genetic relation? I was just telling the wife here about you two, and here's one of you showing up right in front of me." It was Detective Constable Jamieson, come to the rescue.

"And who's this fine lad with you?" he asked.

I turned to Juan and Mary, and found that the gypsy couple had melted into the crowd.

"This is Ian, known as Juan in the states. He is Mack's step-son and has just become a New York City police officer."

"Good for you, lad. You will never be rich, but it's very satisfying work. And the young lady?"

If Detective Constable Jamieson knew Mary, he didn't show it.

Juan spoke up, "I was just telling my new friend Mary from Nairn that we were going back there tonight. Her parents live there, and she would be glad if we could give her a lift."

As we talked, Mary kept looking nervously over her shoulder. I was sure that Detective Constable Jamieson picked up on the body language too, for he said,"We've got plenty of room in the Range Rover, and we're all going in the same direction. Why don't you dismiss your cabbie and come back with us?"

On the way back to Nairn, Juan and Mary sat in the back of the van, chatting quietly. I sat in a jump seat behind Jamieson and his wife, and filled them in about Maria's recovery and her plan to go back to the states. Susie, Jamieson's wife, said, "Doesn't sound like much of a honeymoon to me, even with the excitement of getting shot in the leg."

"No, it wasn't much fun for Maria. She's very understanding. I'm sure Mack will make it up to her when he gets back to the states."

Jamieson said, "So Juan is going back with his mother?" "Yes," I said, "Mack and I are going to stay on for a couple of weeks to see what we can stir up."

"Looks like Juan is more interested in the local lassies than going back to the states."

I glanced back. The couple seemed to be sitting closer.

I said, "I agree, but his leave from the New York City Police Force is almost ended, so he will have to go back anyway."

Jamieson said, *sotto voce*, "Sometimes it takes a good man to straighten a girl out. Ain't that so, Suze?"

His wife smacked him on the shoulder, saying, "Just concentrate on the driving, you."

We didn't take Mary back to her parents' house that night. It was rather late, so I asked her to stay at the hotel with us for one more night. She could sleep in a spare bed in Maria's room, and Mack and I would bunk together and plan the reunion. I was concerned about Mrs. Soames more than anything else.

From what I had read, Alzheimer's sufferers got very disoriented easily, but were a lot better in the morning after a night of rest. They were also uncertain about time, so she might think it was the day Mary first came home from school. So if Juan could pass himself as Ian, a friend from school, it would not appear unusual to her.

I had a feeling that Mary had seen enough of the seamy side of Scotland, and was looking forward to some "down home cooking," or whatever passed for that in this spiceless part of the world. I suspect Juan's good looks and courage may have been a factor in that decision.

Back at the fair, the gypsy grabbed Magda by the arm, growling, "Why did you let her get away? You were supposed to keep her at your side, dependent on you at all times."

"Joe, she wanted to step across the fairway and get a snow cone. How was I…"

"You should have gone with her, you fool. How much of our plans have you told her?"

"Why, none. I did as you instructed: find a young girl using drugs, make her dependent upon me as a friend and supplier, introduce her to a few prostitutes who are visited by men from the oil rigs. I did not expect to see that short man to show up here."

"Well, for your sake, let's hope the girl knows nothing about us and our plans. I will have to tell our friend Leroy Kemp about this."

Chapter 21

"This castle hath a pleasant seat; the air nimbly and sweetly recommends itself unto our gentle senses."
—William Shakespeare

On our way back to Nairn, I saw a sign reading "Welcome to Burning Woods Golf Resort and Condominiums, Brought to You by Macbeth Enterprises."

Something jogged my memory, and I remembered the warning issued by the old Bella Calder at the beach. Did she mean to say "Burning Woods" and my overactive imagination and bad ear made me hear "Birnam Woods"?

Then I remembered that today was the day that Mack had selected to take Maria to visit Cawdor Castle, located near Dunsinane Wood, a great forest. I remembered trying to get my students to appreciate Shakespeare by acting out scenes from Macbeth. They seemed to like the bloody ones best. I also recalled that Birnam Wood was used as camouflage for Malcolm's army before the battle at Dunsinane with Macbeth. So maybe there was something to Bella's warning after all. I decided to head over to Cawdor Castle to see what was going on with Mack and Maria. Just in case I didn't get there in time, I put in a call to Detective Inspector Jamieson.

Meanwhile, Mack was pushing Maria's wheelchair along the stately path leading to Cawdor Castle from the parking lot. As they walked through the woods, listening to the birds singing and flying through the shafts of sunlight that glistened in the glade, they were unaware of a shadowy figure in black moving from tree to tree behind them. As they entered the famed Walled Garden, a maze that replicated the Minotaur's labyrinth in Crete, they were too engrossed in the beauty of the moment to notice that they were being followed. The temperature began to rise in the still, summer air, and Mack began to notice footsteps behind them, crunching in the gravel of the path. When he and Maria stopped, the sound of steps behind them stopped. Mack began to wonder if they were being followed, maybe even stalked, and if so, why? Maria noticed that the wheelchair was moving faster, and she could hear Mack begin to breathe heavily.

"What's wrong, Mack?" she said quietly.

"I'm not sure, but I think we're being followed. Don't worry, I see the exit ahead, and the drawbridge to the castle. Once we get there, we will be surrounded by tourists."

Mack began to move faster, and the footsteps kept pace. As they crossed the drawbridge, he looked back, just in time to catch sight of a police constable emerging from the maze. Mack stopped, and waited for the constable to catch up with them.

As he approached, the constable said, "I hope I haven't alarmed you. We got a call from the station in Nairn that you might need assistance here. A Mr. Cascio called my chief, Detective Constable Jamieson, asking him to get in touch with us. Said you might need someone to show you around."

Chapter 22

The next morning, there was a report on SkyNews TV about a fishing boat that had exploded as it was headed directly for an oil rig off the coast of Scotland. There was a side bar on other incidents involving accidents on boats near the oil drilling rigs.

I got a call from Inspector Detective Jamieson, inviting me to stop by down at the station in Nairn. Juan and I drove down there as soon as we could.

When we entered the station, it looked like a war battle station, with police officers manning computers, going in and out with faxes and other important papers. We were ushered into Jamieson's office as soon as we got there.

"Glad to see you, Cascio. Where is your partner, Macintosh?"

"He's supposed to be on his honeymoon, Detective. By the way, thanks for sending an officer over to ride shotgun while Mack and his bride were visiting Cawdor Castle."

"It turned out to be a false alarm," Jamieson said.

"Yes, I know. I was just going on a hunch. An old biddie said something that alarmed me, and I kind of pushed the panic button."

Jamieson said, gracefully, "Well, as the old saying goes, better to be safe than sorry. But that's not why I called you down here."

"What do you mean?"

"Do you remember the news of that fisherman who was holding out against Laird Gump?"

"Yes, I think I read something about that."

"Well, we just found out that it was his boat blew up. We suspect that was involved in the attack on the oil rig in the North Sea."

"That's strange. Why would he do a thing like that?"

"That's what we're trying to figure out. Look, I know this is irregular, but we are really understaffed here, and I understand you have had some success with investigations of this type. We actually checked with a Captain Hightower in the states, and he vetted you."

"Well, there are many who see us as rank amateurs, but we did get lucky a couple of times."

Jamieson said, "I know that. And perhaps you

underestimate your abilities. After all, you are a couple of college graduates with master's degrees and years of dealing with the good, the bad, and the ugly in the public schools in a country we consider to be just above barbaric, so you might just be qualified to help us out here. We can't pay you, of course, but we would appreciate your help."

"Well, it does look as if we have parallel interests. We met this guy Gump on the golf course the other day, and were not too impressed with him."

Jamieson said, "Sal, here's what I want you to do. Go over to the McLean farm and talk to the man's wife. He hasn't been seen in a couple of days, and we believe that it was his boat that exploded near that oil rig. We can't figure out what he was doing out there."

I looked at Juan, and he smiled in anticipation. I said to Jamieson, "Well, Mack is otherwise occupied at the moment, but Juan here is a bona fide police officer from the states, and he would be glad to assist me."

Jamieson said, "Ah, you have a real copper in the family, eh?"

"Yes, and we're very proud of him."

"Well, go to it, lads, and let me know if you find out anything that might be pertinent."

Chapter 23

The next day, we headed out for the McLean farm. I was becoming acutely aware of the pressure of time, for we had only about a week left before Juan and Maria would be heading back for the states, and I had a feeling that Mack would insist on going with them. While I was feeling confident in my investigative abilities, I felt a little unsure about acting on my own. I was used to Mack's intellectual insights and abilties with research. I was also becoming kind of reliant on the strength and intelligence of Juan. In reality, I was a broken-down, retired, Italian-American with bad knees trying to be a Sherlock Holmes or Dashell Hammett. In short, on my own, I would be in over my head, a Sicilian stranger in a strange land.

The farm looked as if it had seen better days. The farm house itself was in need of shingles and had a sagging roof.

There was a barn, with a single cow and a couple of forlorn chickens scratching in the grass. As we drove up, the front door was opened, and an angry-looking woman came out. She had long, straggly grey-black hair and lined cheeks. She had probably been a real beauty once, but life had treated her harshly. As we got out of the car, she shouted, "Get away, you. I don't want to talk to any more newspaper reporters, or any one else for that matter."

Getting out of the car, I said, "Mrs. Mclean, a friend of yours asked us to stop by, Detective Inspector Jamieson from Nairn."

"Ah, you know that fella, do you? I'm not sure I would call him a friend, but he's not a bad sort. What do you want?"

"This is my associate, Ian, from the states. Jamieson asked us to stop by, see if we could be of any help."

"I don't know if you can help, unless it's to take a club to that bastard Laird Gump."

"Yes, I know about him. But what's more important is what has happened to your husband."

Juan said, "We are worried about him too, M'am."

Mrs. Mclean's shoulders slumped, as if the air had been blown out of her lungs. "Yes, dear, I'm worried about him, too. I haven't seen him in four days, and I think it might have been his boat that was involved in that terrible explosion. If he was going to be out for more than a day or two, he would always call me and let me know."

"Did he ever go fishing near the rigs?" I asked.

"Yes, they would all go out there fishing. The fish were attracted to the stuff the old workers would throw over the side. But my Ian was always very fearful about going too near the rigs. A lot of accidents have happened out there, you know."

"What do you mean?"

"Why just last year, a jet plane from the RAF base near Findhorn crashed into the water not far from one of the oil rigs. Can you imagine what it would have been like if the plane hit the rig?"

Mrs. Maclean was about to say something more, when a man walked around from behind the house. He had a shotgun under his arm, and a brace of rabbits slung over his shoulder. He said, "Need any help, Maeve?"

"No, these fellas are from the states, and are asking after my husband. Detective Constable Jamieson sent them over."

Turning to us, she said, "This is Joseph. He was supposed to go fishing with my husband, but missed the boat. Ian was always impatient. His favorite saying was something about the time and tide waiting for no man."

There was something vaguely familiar about Joseph, but I couldn't quite put my finger on it. Joseph glared at us, and said, "We don't need any more people coming around and bothering us, Maeve, especially tourists from the states."

Mrs. Mclean said, "Joseph has been helping me with the farm for the last few days. You will have to forgive him for being so protective."

I wasn't particularly comfortable with the way that Joseph waved that shotgun around, so I decided it was time for us to take our leave.

I said to Mrs. Mclean, "M'am, I sure hope your husband turns up all right. I'm sorry if we bothered you. If you get any news, Detective Constable Jamieson would be glad to hear from you."

Chapter 24

The Ballad of the Royal Game of Golf

There are laddies will drive ye a ball
To the stream from the farthermost tee,
But you must not think driving is all,
You may shank her, and send her ajar,
Ye may land in the sand or the sea;
And ye're done, sir, ye're not worth a pin,
Take the word that an old man will give,
Always take care to be up on the green!

The old folk are confident, and they boast
That their putting is shrewd and sly;
In a bunker they no good at all,
But to grin and make the sand fly.
And a lassie can putt—any she—

Be she Maggy, or Bessie, or Jean,
But a hook shot's the smart thing for me,
To always take care to be up on the green!

I have played in the frost and the thaw,
I have played since the year thirty-three,
I have played in the rain and the snow,
And I trust I may play till I die;
And I tell ye the truth and not lie,
for I speak of the thing I have seen—
Tom Morris, I ken, will agree—
Always take care to be up on the green!

—By Andrew Lang, 1844-1912
(loose translation by the author)

A few days later, Mack and Maria took a cab to the Pringle outlet store. Mack wanted to get a kilt in the Macintosh tartan, or something close to it. If you can imagine a stork dressed in a plaid skirt, you might get an idea of what he would look like, but he was really into this Scottish heritage thing, and I couldn't deter him.

Juan and Mary Soames, who had been spending some time together lately, had decided to go kayaking on the Findhorn River, so I was left to my own resources.

I decided I would take a look at the golf course being built by Laird Gump. I had heard that the first nine holes were finished and open for play. Gump couldn't go any further until he solved the problem of the Mclean farm. I couldn't imagine Mrs. Mclean holding out against him now.

I drove through imposing gates and up a sweeping drive bordered by the ubiquitous Scottish roses to a clubhouse that looked like a small castle, replete with leaded windows and turrets with flags flying. A sturdy fellow in a kilt took my golf bag from the car, and offered to park for me. I went in to see if I could register and play a few holes. A comely lass in a ruffled blouse and, of course, a short kilt, took my information and credit card, saying, "Are you meeting anyone, sir? Or are you hoping to join a group?"

I told her I had heard about the course and wanted to try it out, even if it wasn't finished. I said I represented a firm in the states that was looking for an appropriate setting for the annual board of directors' meeting. At that mention, she picked up a telephone and called an office.

She said, "I think Mr. Gump would like to meet with you. Would you wait here just a minute?"

Shortly the great man himself came through a pair of swinging doors, golden locks flowing. He was dressed for golf. He looked at me, frowning quizzically. "You look familiar. Have we met before?"

I said, "Our paths crossed briefly about a week ago on the

course at Nairn. We invited you to play through, as we were having trouble finding our way."

"Well, that kind of thing wouldn't happen here. We have the latest in motorized golf carts, each equipped with a GPS system that tells you the distance to the hole from anywhere in the fairway, even how much time you should be spending on each hole."

"That's impressive, sir."

"Yes, we're very pleased with it." He paused, then said, "Look, we had a foursome, but one of the fellows didn't show up. Would you care to join us? I am sorry we will only be able to play nine holes, but I am expecting to finish the course pretty soon. I think you will find the first nine so well laid out that your group will enjoy their stay here."

I accepted his invitation, and there followed the strangest game of golf I would ever play. The two fellows playing with us were right out of central casting. One, a Jose Cortez, was a gentleman from Colombia, a Chi Chi Rodriguez dressed in immaculate white. The other player reminded me of Paulie Walnuts from the HBO hit, "The Sopranoes." I wouldn't want to meet either of them in a dark alley, in Bogota, Colombia, or Bogota, New Jersey. The New Jersey guy's name was Beefy Johnson.

Before we teed off, Gump said, "Why don't we make this interesting. How about a little betting?"

There followed a discussion about the different kinds of

bets we could make. We couldn't make the Nassau three bets in one, of course, as it called for low score on the front nine, low score on the back nine, and low score over the full 18 holes. We discussed the merits of other kinds of scoring: Sandies, where a golfer automatically wins the bet either by making par on a hole in which he was in a sand trap, or by getting up and down from a greenside bunker; Barkies, sometimes called Woodies, paid automatically to any player who makes par on a hole on which he hit a tree; Aces and Deuces, a bet in which there is a winner, two modest losers, and one biggest loser on each hole; Gruesomes, which pits two-person teams against each other, both members tee off, then the other team gets to choose which of the drives your side has to play; Criers and Whiners, a game of mulligans for those players who are always crying and whining about that handful of shots they screwed up; and Wolf, one of the classic golf betting games for groups of four, where players rotate as the "wolf," and on each side the player designated as the wolf has to choose whether to play 1 against 3, or 2 on 2. The Wolf can win or lose more money by going it alone.

While he clearly qualified for the game of Criers and Whiners, Laird Gump chose to be the Wolf. I was not surprised.

The other two players were clearly not happy with any form of the game. I got the impression they had agreed to play only to please the Laird. They looked even more uncomfortable when the Laird proposed a complicated progressive form of betting, where the bets doubled after each hole. We started with a five dollar bet going to the winner of the first hole. That could be doubled on the second, tripled on the third, and so forth. It seemed innocent at first, but if someone lost the ninth hole, he could lose $1280. Do the math. Or if someone won every hole, he could win $2555.

As we went from hole to hole, a pattern began to develop. Beefy and Jose were terrible golfers, and didn't win a hole. The Laird and I seemed to be pretty much on a par. We kept trading off holes.

Beefy had a real problem controlling his temper. He had a tendency to hit his ball into the trees bordering one side of the course. Each time he went into the woods, he would return without a club. I watched him the last time this happened. He flubbed his shot, then wrapped the club around the nearest tree, showing prodigious strength. He stumped back out onto the course, dropped a ball, and selected another club from his dwindling supply.

Jose, on the other hand, slashed at his ball as if he were wielding a sword. He seemed to have an affinity for the bunkers that surrounded each hole, and every time I looked at him, he was swinging away in a cloud of sand and dust, regardless of whose turn it was.

The Laird was the one I had to really watch, for he seemed

intent on winning all the bets, at any cost. When I prepared to drive, he would jingle the coins in his pocket or cough loudly. Several times, I caught him kicking his ball into a better lie, and had to call him out on it. The worst thing was that I had to keep track of his strokes as well as mine.

Another distraction was the man's incessant chatter. He seemed to want to know my life history: where I was married, why I was not with my wife, why I retired from teaching, what I was doing in Scotland. Especially what I was doing in Scotland. He seemed to believe my story of coming to a friend's aid, but I wasn't sure. After all, this guy was one of the titans of the American real estate and financial world, and dealing with a small fry like a retired school teacher must have been like shooting fish in the proverbial barrel for him.

By the end of our nine-hole outing, I was exhausted, not from the game but from his barrage of questions. Of course, he won most of the money.

Chapter 25

As it was Maria and Juan's last day in Scotland, Mack and I decided to make it a festive sending away party. We got reservations at a seaside restaurant in Nairn that looked over the stately river as it coursed towards the Firth of Moray. The traveling circus had returned to the park by the beach. Crowds of happy fairgoers marched to and from concessions, like "Auden's fields of summer wheat." The air was filled with brassy music and screams of excitement from the rides. There was a sparkle in Maria's cheeks as the men in her life waited on her hand and foot. She was no longer in a wheelchair, but a throne, a royal chariot, and we were her loyal servants.

After a sumptuous feast of mussels, clams, langostinos, Dover sole, and several bottles of fine white wine, we decided to get some fresh air by taking in the sights at the fair.

Here and there, I noticed pockets of what looked like gypsy booths: fortune telling, games of chance, guess your weight, age, and so forth. There was one that had attracted a large crowd. The sign proclaimed, "Win 200 euros by lasting 5 minutes in the ring with the Romani Strongman!" Standing in the center of the mat was my old friend Joseph from the Mclean farm.

As we neared the ring, a voice called out from the crowd, "Here you go, Yanks! Think you can last five minutes with a gypsy?"

Mack said, "What is this? Boxing? I don't see any gloves."

The hawker said, "Nah, we don't go by any fancy Marquis of Queensbury rules here, mate. The gypsy's favorite sport is wrestling, dint' ya know?"

I don't know what made me respond. Maybe it was the excessive amounts of wine at dinner, maybe it was the stinging loss of over $1,000 in my ill-advised game with the Laird. Maybe I was just a stupid, broken-down Sicilian with bad knees who used to be a pretty good wrestler. Pretty good? I was undefeated in my senior year at college, captain of the team, had almost made it at the Olympic tryouts. Forget the fact of my advanced age, forget the bad knees. I was 21 again, ready to go into battle. Call me crazy. You're right.

Mack said, "Sal, are you sure you want to do this? He looks like a rough customer."

Juan spoke up, "Maybe I should be the one to fight him. After all, I am a little younger than you, Sal."

Maria looked worried, but didn't say anything. Her eyes implored me to stay out of the ring.

What Maria and Juan did not know is that after wrestling for eight years in high school and college combined, I had gone on to coach wrestling for 25 years during my teaching career, resulting in moves ingrained by hours of practice on the mat. They say that there is something called muscle memory, and as Joseph and I circled each other in the ring before the howling crowd, I could feel little twinges coming from long-unused parts of my body.

We came together in a rush, and I could feel his strength and smell the sweat of his unwashed body. I automatically dropped into a fireman's carry take down, seeming to drop before his superior strength, then grabbing his elbow and far knee, ducking down, and throwing him on the mat. The breath went out of his lungs with a loud "whoosh." I knew I had to take care of him quickly, for I would not last more than a few minutes against his superior strength and age advantage. I quickly put my legs across his upper leg behind the knee in a figure four, reached behind his back, and pulled his arm and head into a grip called "the crucifix." This grip is exceedingly painful, as it twists the spine. The more the victim struggles, the tighter and more painful the hold. I held Joseph in this uncomfortable position for five minutes, as he cursed me in several different languages. Every once in awhile, I gave his head a little squeeze, and he grunted in pain. Soon, the time was up, and I had won my 200 euros. As Joseph sat on the mat, glaring up at me, I realized I had also won an enemy.

Chapter 26

Early the next morning, we all piled into the rental car to take Maria and Juan to the airport in Glasgow. We would be stopping in Edinburgh for one last look at Robert Burns' statue and a bit of breakfast before heading west to Glasgow.

On the drive over to Glasgow, I gave a short dissertation on the differences between the two cities: the lasting image of Glasgow as a vast, industrial slum, a vicious place populated by gangsters, loyal but downtrodden housewives, sluttish but well-meaning mistresses, and domestic tyrants of all ages. None of it true, however, as that city has become an economic powerhouse. Edinburgh, on the other hand, has always been portrayed as a city of arts and letters, a mythical city of restraint and denial. When I think of Edinburgh, I think of a character created by Alexander McColl Smith, one Isabel Dalhousie, featured in such delightful mysteries as *The Right Attitude to Rain*, *44 Scotland Street*, and *The Careful Use of Compliments*. Isabel, a well-do-do, somewhat nosy editor of a philosopical journal, explores the rights and wrongs of everyday life.

Mack said, "Sal, you never cease to amaze me. Yesterday, you were rolling around in the dirt with a gypsy, and today you're talking about moral philosophy."

I said, "Oh, I'm just a Renaissance man."

Chapter 27

As Mack, Sal, Maria, and Juan headed for Glasgow, they were followed by a black Mercedes sedan. There were two men inside: the driver was one Joseph Caddy, still smarting from the beating administered by an older, smaller man. The other was a big, florid American, an exporter of fine Scotch whiskey.

"Do you think they know we're following them?" said the American.

"No, they are too involved in sightseeing and each other to be aware of us. That's the way it is with Americans. They see everything through a clouded lens, their own distorted vision of their importance in the world."

"Well, I have a score to settle with those two, so keep after them."

"As I do, my friend, but this time when I get close to the little fellow, I will have a knife in my hand."

"All right, let's just do the job we have been assigned today. Just keep after them, find out where they go, and whether they all go."

Caddy said, "I think it is only two that are leaving. I have a little friend who works as a maid in their hotel. She said that only the woman and her son have checked out. The other two appear to be staying on for awhile."

"That's odd. The man and woman were supposed to be on a honeymoon. Maybe their ardour has cooled."

Chapter 28

After saying farewell to Maria and Juan, we got in the car and started back on the A9 for Nairn by way of Inverness. As we drove north, Mack said, "Don't look now, but I think we are being followed."

"What? Where?" I looked in the rear vision mirror, and saw a black Mercedes several cars back.

"Do you think it's the same car?" I asked.

Mack said, "Well, it's a black Mercedes in a country full of Rolls Royces, and it has a distinctive thistle emblem on its front license plate. I noticed the thistle."

"Well, let's see if they follow us all the way back to Nairn," I said.

Sure enough, the car tailed us all the way through Inverness, neglecting to turn off at several roundabouts on either side of the city. As we headed for Nairn, I said, "I think I know of a way to shake them."

A number of years ago, I had been cut off when entering the Long Island Expressway. Reacting without thinking, I flipped the bird to the offending driver in a universal hand signal of contempt. He did not take my gesture lightly, for he proceeded to follow me down the expressway, waving his fist and gesticulating for me to stop so we could have it out. He looked like the kind of burly fellow who keeps a tire iron under his front seat, so I chose not to engage him. Sometimes discretion is truly more important than valor. The guy continued to follow me down the expressway, at one point giving me a shove with his front bumper, which at 70 miles an hour could be a dangerous maneuver to anyone. Shortly I pulled off at the Yaphank Avenue exit, which led directly to the headquarters of the Suffolk County Police Department. I had a few friends there, and I knew they would intercede for me if the occasion arose. As I pulled into the police headquarters parking lot, I looked over my shoulder. My angry friend roared away, shaking his fist at me.

Pulling into Nairn, we did not go to the hotel, but headed directly to the center of town, and pulled up in front of the police station. I turned around to see our followers, but they had disappeared.

Mack said, "I guess they lost interest in us."

I answered, "No, but they don't want to hang around the police station either. Let's go in and see if our friend Detective Inspector Jamieson is in."

The Inspector was in, beseiged by faxes, reports, and an annoying telephone call. He ran his hand through a thick head of hair, saying, "Yes, I wish we could help you right away, M"am. Yes, I understand it is a terrible thing for someone to steal your laundry off the line. No, I don't think it was the gypsies. Yes, we will send someone out as soon as possible. But you have to understand, it is holiday season and we are terrible short-staffed as it is. Yes, yes, we will be there as soon as possible."

He sighed and slammed the phone down.

Mack said, "I see you have your hands full, Don. Should we come back at another time?"

Jamieson said, "No, no, our laundry bandits can wait. What's been happening with you fellows? I heard you had a bit of a dust-up with some gypsy at the fair, Cascio."

He looked at me with a bit of respect, adding, "And you don't seem any worse for the experience."

We told him about our visit to the Mclean farm, and the handyman who turned out to be my wrestling opponent. Jamieson said, "Well, I'm sure you've heard the saying, 'There are no coincidences.'"

Mack said, "Yes, that seemed strange to us, too."

I went on to tell the Inspector about my golf game with the Laird and his strange associates. He said, "You got to play golf with Laird Gump? You sure do get around, Cascio. Tell me about the fellows who played with you. What were their names again? You say one was from Latin America and the other from the states?"

I told him as much as I could about Cortez and Johnson, and he said, "I will feed those names into our Interpol computer. Maybe we will get lucky."

Then we told him about the car that had followed us back from Glasgow. "That's a considerable distance. You think it followed you over there too. Someone must be very interested in your activities."

"Looks that way," said Mack.

Jamieson said, "Look, I want you fellows to be careful. It won't look good for our tourism business if a couple of Yanks get wiped out on a golf holiday. But I do have something you might be in a position to help us with."

Mack smiled, then said, "Let us have it, Cuz."

Jamieson said, "There's an American new to the area, claiming to be in the whiskey exporting business. We checked him out, because that is a sensitive area. We couldn't get much information from the trade association. Maybe you two could nose around, stir things up a bit, help us out."

"Sure," said Mack. "We won't be playing golf all the time. What's his name?"

"Leroy Kemp," said Detective Inspector Jamieson.

Getting over our surprise, we had a few things to say about Leroy Kemp: how the disgraced football coach/

school board member had used his players, Fagin-like, to smuggle drugs on Long Island; how he had worked as a front for the Colombian drug cartel, funneling illegal money into a golf resort; how we believed he had masterminded the murders of a couple of innocent brothers, and then had some of his underlings mount a near-fatal attack on Mack, and a followup attempt on the rest of us.

"This is an ambitious guy," I said to Jamieson. "I'm surprised he hasn't been brought to ground by now. There must be a warrant out for his arrest."

Mack said, "Yes, but I think the authorities are looking in the wrong direction. They probably think he fled to Colombia and the protection of his drug overlords. Who would think to look for him way up here? Doesn't Scotland have an extradition agreement with the United States?"

"Yes, we do, of course," said Jamieson, "but the paperwork will take some time."

I said, "Knowing who he is, can't you just throw him in jail until the papers come through?"

"No," said Jamieson, "this isn't the states, where that kind of thing seems to be happening lately. We are not suffering from the same paranoia, you know."

Mack said, "So what can we do?"

Jamieson answered, "Well, you can't do anything illegal, of course. But you two can continue to do the thing you do best. You seem to attract trouble, and maybe by just being yourselves, sticking your nose where it doesn't always belong, maybe you can stir things up a bit."

Mack said, "Yes, I think we can do that for the remaining weeks of our holiday."

Chapter 29

It was our last night in Scotland, or so we thought. Since our meeting with Detective Inspector Jamieson, we had not turned up anything new. We did, however, find out that the Mclean farm had been sold and razed. We had gone out there to see if there were any new developments, and to see if that Caddy fellow was still hanging around. When we turned into the road leading to the farm, we found it was blocked by a gate and a security guard. In the background, where the farmhouse once stood, there was a pile of rubble being pushed about by a bulldozer. The cow was gone, as were the few remaining chickens. I leaned out the window and said, "Say, can you tell us what has happened here? Has the place been sold?"

The guard didn't say anything. He just pointed to a sign, which read, "Under Development, Laird Enterprises."

So it looks like the Ugly American had gotten his way after all. Mack said, "I wonder what's next—a Battle of Culloden Theme Park?"

We had decided to have dinner at the Firthside with the Jamiesons. After a long evening of a lot of stories and glasses of Scotch, we bade farewell to the Jamiesons with promises to stay in touch. Mack went to the computer room to send an e-mail to Maria, and I decided to step out for an after-dinner cigar. The sun was setting in the west as I strolled out along the cart path leading to the first tee of the old Nairn golf course, situated on a little promontory that juts out into the firth. As I stood looking out at the fishing boats coming into the harbor, I heard a sound behind me. I turned, and found three men approaching. It was Caddy, holding a knife in one hand and a canvas knapsack over his shoulder. On one side, stood Beefy Johnson, fitting what looked like brass knuckles to his hands. On Caddy's other side stood Señor Cortez, holding some kind of club. The night had suddenly turned cold, and I felt a shiver run up my spine.

Caddy said, "I told you we would meet again, my short friend. This time there are no police about to intercede. Which would you like first—a beating or a stabbing?"

He stepped forward, waving the knife in my face. Suddenly the quiet evening air, so full of menace, was shattered by a piercing howl, a barbaric yawp that would have done Walt Whitman proud. The three desperados facing me spun around, only to be confronted by a creature from hell, a long-legged banshee emerging from the semi-darkness, white knees flashing under a kilt, swinging a mashie with such force that Caddy's knife went spinning out over the water. It was Rob Roy, William Wallace, Bonnie Prince Charlie himself come to do battle with the forces of evil. Mack spun around, waving the club at the other two attackers while Caddy fell to his knees, holding a shattered wrist. The canvas bag dropped to the ground at his side, and I kicked it out of the way, thinking it might contain more weapons. The golf club bounced off the head of Beefy Johnson, dropping him to the ground like a pole-axed steer. Cortez gripped his club, and took aim at Mack's head. I took my cigar and threw it in his face, catching him between the eyes with a shower of sparks and hot ashes. He dropped the club and screamed, holding his eyes.

Shortly, other guests came running out from the hotel, along with our friend Jamieson, who had doubled back after a call went out over the police radio.

As he put our attackers in handcuffs, Jamieson said, "Only two, Sal. I thought you were attacked by three men here."

I looked over as our would-be attackers were loaded into a police lorry.

"Where's the gypsy?" I asked.

Sure enough, the elusive Joseph Caddy had slipped away in the night.

Chapter 30

> Finders Keepers, Losers, Weepers.
> —Child's rhyme

Later in the evening, after all the excitement had died down, I went back out to the promontory. Looking in the bushes on either side, I soon found the canvas knapsack I had kicked out of the way. I picked it up, went back to the hotel, and knocked on Mack's door.

"What have you got there, Sal" he said.

"Caddy, that gypsy guy, dropped this in the attack. I think you might find the contents interesting."

The bag was full of tightly wrapped bank notes, bricks and bricks of euros. We estimated the haul in the amount of about a million.

Mack whistled after we had added up the loot, and said, "Well, this places us under a classic moral dilemma, doesn't it?"

"What do you mean?" I asked.

Mack said, "Well, let's think about who the money belongs to. It's illegal drug money, no doubt, so it probably was in the temporary custody of our gypsy friend. I'm not sure about the law here, but if drug money were seized in the United States, it would become the property of the government, the way they take a drug dealer's houses, cars, boats. Now, here's the dilemma. Nobody knows, except maybe Caddy, that we have the money. Now that he knows the police are on to him, he probably wants to get out of the country as quickly as possible."

"That's right, but we can't just give all the money to the Scottish authorities."

"I think I have an answer to our dilemma," said Mack.

Chapter 31

Our departure was delayed by a couple of days as we filled out reports for the police. Two of my attackers, Johnson and Cortez, would be held until they could be deported back to their respective countries as "undesirable aliens."

It turned out that the unpleasant Laird Gump would have his way, after all. Mrs. Mclean had finally given in and sold her property to the developer, so the Laird would have his castle in Scotland after all. Sometimes the bad guys win. As for his association with Johnson and Cortez, it seems they were prospective investors in his scheme, looking to probably place illegal assets in a respectable business venture.

Jamieson said, "This Laird fellow is indeed a nasty piece of work, associating with known criminals. But we can't put him in jail for the company he keeps, you know."

He was delighted when we turned in a canvas knapsack containing a half a million in euros. "Mack, your suggestion is excellent. This money will be donated to our widows and orphans fund, and make a lot of people happy. Where did you say you found it?"

Nothing was heard from Caddy or Kemp, until a report from Interpol came in to Jamieson's office. The Detective Inspector summarized it for us, saying, "Caddy and this fellow Kemp were seen boarding the Flying Scot, a high-speed train from Edinburgh to London. Kemp has been using his credit card, and from London, their movements were traced to Plymouth, where they hired a boat to take them to France. Looks like they are on the run, but why? There's more to this than Caddy's attack on you. It would appear that Kemp was behind the attack, but why? Why expose himself to the local authorities?"

Mack thought he found the answer to that question when he picked up a copy of the *Aberdeen Times* at the newsstand. The lead article had the following headline: "Threats to Oil Industry, Offshore Drilling in Peril"

According to the article, recent attacks on oil rigs and other acts of sabotage, coupled with the increase of drug use among oil workers, has had an deleterious effect on the Scottish oil and gas industry, so much so, that the price of oil has been affected. The laws of supply and demand were coming into play, and many of Scotland's customers were looking to the Middle East and South America for oil.

We stopped by the police station, and found that Jamieson had read the same newspaper. He said, "This looks like a big problem, one that affects the well-being of the Scottish economy. My superiors have instructed me to step up our investigation."

Mack said, "Don, we have a little time and money available, and we plan to follow Kemp to France. Would you like to join us? It wouldn't hurt to have someone with official credentials with us."

Jamieson said, "Now I see why you fellows got such a good recommendation from the police in the states. They said you worked well with the local authorities, and in fact, helped to solve a couple of cases. I have some vacation time coming up, so why don't we take a little trip to France?"

Chapter 32

The trip was touted to one and all as a boys' week in Paris, a chance for two cousins to do a little male bonding. Fortunately, we had a little traveling money at our disposal.

We decided to fly from Glasgow to Paris, gaining on the fugitives by a day or so. Landing at Charles DeGaulle Airport, we were met by one Inspector Henri Belber, our liaison with the French authorities. His English was better than our high school French, so he brought us up to date as we drove into Paris.

He said, "It would appear, my friends, that your fugitives have arrived in Paris. They do not seem to be disguising their identities, in fact, they are traveling quite openly, using a credit card, and leaving their passports at the hotels."

"Why haven't you picked them up?" said Mack.

"Well, sir, there's the rub, as you would say in Scotland.

They are like *les puces*, fleas, hopping quickly from hotel to hotel. We hear they are in one place. Once we go there, we find they have checked out. I do not understand why they are using a credit card. It is like a beacon in the night."

We told the inspector why the fugitives had to use a credit card, that we had their cash.

"Perhaps this would be a way to lure them into a trap," said Inspector Belber, scratching his unshaven chin.

"But how can we anticipate where they are going next?" said Jamieson.

Belber said, "Let's look at the hotels where they have stayed, maybe there will be a pattern."

He took out a map of Paris, which had been marked with a series of red x's, the first being at a small hotel near the Gare St. Lazare.

Mack said, "It looks like they came to Paris from the northeast, which makes sense. We know they took a boat from Plymouth to Normandy."

I looked at the map. The next mark indicated a Best Western near the Arch de Triomphe. The next night, they evidently stopped in the St. Michel area.

Inspector Belber said, "We think they are making their way towards the Algerian section of town."

Jamieson said, "That would make sense. There are gypsies living there, too, and perhaps Caddy is looking for a friendly face."

Belber said, "I have a plan to help us catch our *puces*. We have some informants living in the Algerian quarter, and if we had the right bait, we could draw our fugitives out into the open."

Mack said, "Sal and I have some bait. We have Caddy's money, almost half a million in cash. Do you think that would be enough to draw him out into the open?"

"Certainment, mon ami," said Belber.

Chapter 33

So the word went out along the underworld network: If a certain gypsy wanted to retrieve money lost in Scotland, he should bring his American friend to Pere-Lachaise Cemetery at 2:00 p.m. Saturday. He would get the money if and when he handed over the American, a fugitive from justice.

"Do you think this will work?" I asked Belber. "It seems kind of obvious."

"Yes, my friend, perhaps because it is so obvious. We know that their present plan is going to catch up with them soon. There is also the expression that there is 'no honor among thieves.' Caddy needs his money if he is to escape. He will work out a way to do so."

Later that week, Mack and I found ourselves wandering along the paths of Pere-Lachaise, final resting place of such luminaries as Balzac, Sarah Bernhardt, Colette, Oscar Wilde, Jim Morrison, and those ill-fated lovers, Heloise and Abelard, along with legions of resident cats. It was a weekend, and the place was crawling with tourists.

"Maybe this wasn't such a good idea," said Mack. We had left Jamieson and Inspector Belber at the gate, and neglecting to get a map, were now thoroughly lost.

"We need to find Morrison's grave," I said. "That's where the money is supposed to be handed over."

Mack said, "As they say in the detective business, 'follow the money.' Now, if we can only find where it's supposed to be."

As we turned a corner, there were spitting sounds, "Pfft! Pfft!" and a concrete angel disintegrated just over our heads.

"Whoa!" Mack yelled, ducking behing a tombstone. There were more spitting sounds, and I felt a stinging sensation in my arm. I jumped behind the tombstone with Mack.

"This is not good," he said. Our plan had backfired, no pun intended, and the hunters had become the hunted.

A familiar voice called out, "Mack? Sal? I know you're over there. Just leave the money, and we will let you go."

Mack yelled, "Not a chance, Leroy. You know we're not alone here. The others will be along any minute now, and you will be outnumbered. Why don't you give yourself up?"

Kemp's answer was another shot that took a bite out of the stone protecting us.

He yelled, "There are two of us, and we both have guns. We will get to you before your friends can come to the rescue."

Just then, a horde of Bavarian tourists came down the path, chattering away. They were led by the ubiquitous guide holding an unfurled umbrella high in the air.

Mack said, "Here's our chance." He jumped out, inserting himself between a couple of bovine *haus fraus* on holiday from Munich. I wrapped my jacket around my injured arm and joined him.

We found our inspectors at the gate and told them what had happened. I had lost some blood by then, and was beginning to feel a little woozy.

Inspector Belber said, "We had better get you to the hospital, Sal. Our fugitives have obviously seen through our little plan."

Mack said,"Yes, and they know that we are still on their trail."

Chapter 34

It took a few days for me to recover from the flesh wound in my arm. By then, we were sure, the fugitives were off and running again. There were no further reports of their checking in to any hotels in Paris. Then Jamieson got another report from Interpol. Caddy and Kemp had been seen crossing the border into Spain, and had stayed in a hotel on the *Ramblas* in Barcelona. From there, they had taken a plane to Grenada, and evidently, dropped off the face of the earth.

Bidding farewell to Inspectors Belber and Jamieson, Mack and I booked a flight to Malaga.

The next night, we checked into the parador in the fabled Alhambra in Grenada. After dinner that night, we strolled along the battlements, looking across the valley at the gypsy campfires blazing in front of hillside caves.

Mack said, "They call them 'trogdolytes' over here, you know?"

I said, "Makes sense, since they're living in caves. I understand some of the caves even have electricity and running water."

The sounds of laughter and flamenco music wafted across the valley in the night air.

Meanwhile, standing in front of one of those caves, a gypsy looked across the valley at the Alhambra. He said to the large, florid man next to him, "This is where we part company, my friend. I am with my people, and they will take care of me. The local authorities tolerate us here, but do not bother us. To them, I am just another gypsy living in a cave."

Kemp said, "Well, we have given the bastards a run for their money, eh?"

"What are you going to do?" said Caddy.

"Best that you not know, Joseph. However, I can tell you that I have managed to get in touch with my friends in Colombia, and they still have a need for my services."

Chapter 35

The next day, Mack and I were driving our rental back to Malaga, where we would catch a British Air flight back to London and eventually the states. As we entered Malaga, we stopped at a traffic light. I looked at the car next to us, a large black limousine. Suddenly, I found myself staring at Leroy Kemp! He stared back, his mouth hanging open in surprise. Then he yelled something at his driver, and the limo shot forward. I hit the gas, jumping out in pursuit.

Mack yelled, "What's going on?" Apparently he had been dozing during the long drive down from Grenada.

"I just saw Kemp!" I shouted.

There followed a high-speed chase, right out of the movies. Kemp had a pretty good driver, and we were barely able to keep up with him.

We roared into the port town of Algeceris. Obviously

Kemp was headed for Africa, for several ferries sailed between Algeceris and Tangiers.

Kemp was just a few minutes ahead of us, but that was enough time for him to leap out of the limo and run for a ferry that was just departing. He jumped aboard just as they pulled up the gangplank, and the high-speed ferry moved out into the Mediterranean. We pulled up and stood on the dock, watching the departing ship in frustration. A lone figure in a white suit stood on the afterdeck, waving a straw hat in a mocking gesture of farewell.

Mack said, "I wonder if this is, in fact, the last we will see of Leroy Kemp."

Chapter 36

As we watched the ferry disappear over the horizon, Mack said, "Well, there he goes."

I said, "We have a choice. Either we stay here in Spain and try to find Joe Caddy, or we go after Kemp in the wilds of North Africa."

Mack said, "Or we go home to America, with our tails between our legs. I hate to give up on the chase, but to tell the truth, all this international travel is getting a bit expensive."

"You forget that we are traveling on Joe Caddy's money, and I still have a few gold doubloons stashed in the safety deposit box back home. We're O.K. for traveling money."

"Well, if that's the case, I say we go for it. Maria's going to kill me, but this is the kind of adventure we only read about when we were teaching."

"As the poet said, 'carpe diem.' Let's go for it. Now, which way? North or south?"

Mack thought for a moment, then said, "I say we go south. Caddy is going to be hard to find, now that he's among his people."

With that decision, we turned in the rental car at Avis, and bought two tickets to the next ferry. We should have paid more attention, for the ferry ride was much shorter than we had anticipated. As we got off the boat, an official checked our passports. I said to him, "That was a short ride."

"No, señor, not any shorter than usual. Welcome to Spanish Ceutas."

"Ceutas?" I said, "I thought this was the ferry for Tangiers."

"No, señor, this is Spanish Ceutas. And the next ferry for Algeceris will not leave until tomorrow morning."

Talk about babes in the woods. In our eagerness to get on with the chase, we had not looked carefully at the signs in the ferry terminal, and had taken the wrong boat.

I said to the official, "We wanted to go to Tangiers."

He said, with a patient smile, as if dealing with ignorant Americans was something he did every day, "Well, señor, if you can get across the border, you can take a taxi to Tangiers. It is just on the other side of the mountains."

We went to a money exchange, and cashed in some euros for something called "dirham," the money used in Morocco.

The proprietor of the money exchange told us if we were going to Tangiers we should engage the services of an "expeditor," in fact his cousin, who for the miniscule sum of 300 *dirham* would help us get through customs and border officials.

Arrangements were made, and we crossed the border into Morocco, looking nervously at armed guards and huddled refugees on each side of the border. When we reached the other side, our expeditor said, "You want to go to Tangiers, right?"

Without waiting for an answer, he said, "I have a cousin, he will take you to Tangiers for 300 dirham."

It seemed that 300 *dirham* was the going rate for everything, these days. We followed our guide to a row of ancient Mercedes, and after a heated discussion, he handed us over to a driver, who kicked an old lady out of the front seat of the sedan.

"Who is that?" Mack asked our guide.

He said, "Oh, that is his mother. She will wait for him here until he returns."

So off we went, in a cloud of dust and diesel exhaust fumes, up and over the Atlas Mountains. In many places, the road was washed out, and we had to take a detour. The circuitous route took us through many small towns, and at each case, we had to stop at the local police station, where the driver would present our passports and a few *dirham*.

We asked the driver why he had to make so many stops, but he just shrugged his shoulders and said, "For securite, you know. There are a lot of terrorists about." His English was not much better than my high school French, so we lapsed into long periods of silence, watching the peasants as they drove their heavily-laden donkeys towards town.

After an eight-hour ride, we pulled up to the outer limits of Tangiers. Our driver stopped the car, and he held the door for us with one hand, and the other extended for payment.

Mack said, "Wait. We want to go to the port of Tangiers. This is the other side of town."

The cab driver shrugged, then said, "I take you to Tangiers. This is Tangiers. I do not have license to drive in the city."

Then he relented, and said, "I will call you Tangiers taxi."

Chapter 37

About a half an hour later, another taxi appeared in a cloud of dust.

A few more dirham exchanged hands, and our first driver left, no doubt on his way back to the border and his mother.

Our new driver, a lean fellow with a mouthful of broken and missing teeth, said, "Where are you going?"

I named the only hotel I had heard about in Tangiers, the fabled Hotel Continental.

As we drove through the crowded streets of the medina, Mack said, "Where did you hear about this hotel?"

I told him what I knew about the hotel, about how it was celebrated in 1950's literature as a hang-out for American and British ex-patriates like Paul Bowles, William Burroughs, Jack Kerouac, Allen Ginsberg, and Tennessee Williams, back when Tangiers was notorious for its free and easy way of life, and ready access to drugs and sex in all of its varied forms. Winston Churchill had stayed at the Hotel Continental, and it had been used as the locale for two films, "The Sheltering Sky" and the first Indiana Jones film.

I said, "I don't know why, but I have a hunch that's where Kemp is headed."

Mack said, "Why?"

I said,"I looked in the guide book, and it says the Hotel Continental overlooks the port, and is the nearest hotel."

Mack said, "So you've been doing your homework. Maybe you're right."

He thought for a minute, then said, "Speaking of hunches, I've got to tell you I'm beginning to have a funny feeling about this chase."

"What do you mean?"

"Well, did it ever occur to you that we might be involved in a wild goose chase, that Kemp is leading us into a trap?"

"How can that be? Does he even know we are on his trail?"

Mack said, looking out at the crowded streets of the soukh, "After that attack in Paris, it occurred to me that they might want to get their money back, but they couldn't get it until we were out of the protective umbrella cast by our friends in the Scottish and French police. They had to get us out here in the open, to take another crack at us."

Suddenly our excursion to Morocco did not seem like

such a good idea after all. Maybe the hunters were about to become the hunted, a rabbit with fangs.

We finally pulled up to the back gate of the Hotel Continental. The driver blew his horn several times, and an old porter pulled the faded, blue gate open to let the cab into the courtyard.

Entering the hotel, we realized that the place had seen better days. The rugs were frayed, the table tops were dusty, and there was a general air of decay about the hotel. We were met at the front desk by an unctuous clerk who greeted us effusively.

"Ah, from America?" he said, "you are the second visitor this week from the United States. How wonderful."

Mack said, "May we know the name of the other visitor?"

The clerk looked in the register and said, "A Mr. Kemp. Leroy Kemp, from New York. But he left yesterday afternoon."

Mack looked at me and said, "So close, and so far. Looks like your hunch was right."

I said, "Well, I hope that was the only correct hunch."

We decided to stay for the night, then head down the hill to the port and return to Algeceris.

Our rooms were on the top floor, with a great view of the city, its mosques, and the port. That was about all it had going for it, however. When we looked at the lumpy mattresses, the torn sheets, and the cockroaches scurrying about the bathrooms, we wondered if we had made the right decision.

"Well, it's only for one night," Mack said. "I think I will take a shower before we get some dinner."

He quickly changed his mind when he turned on the water and a stream of yellow-brown liquid flowed from the tap.

"Maybe I'll pass on the shower," he said.

The hotel restaurant was only open for breakfast, so we had to get a porter from the hotel to guide us through the maze known as the *soukh* to a restaurant of any note.

The poverty of the place was incredible, as craftsmen worked at the entrance of their one-room domiciles. Street urchins dogged our heels, begging for a handout.

We got to the restaurant, and had a decent meal. After supper, one of the waiters led us back through the *soukh*. We walked out on the terrace of the hotel and looked down on a disused garden. Mack said, "This place must have been a grand old lady in her time. It's too bad it has gone to seed. I think I'm going to stay up for awhile. All that tea with supper has me wired."

I said,"Well, it had the opposite effect on me. I'm turning in."

Mack said, looking at the garden in the moonlight, "I think I will try to put in a call to Maria. Let her know we're heading home. What time is it now in the states? Sometime in the morning, I think. Any message for Carol?"

On our travels, we had learned that Carol had returned to Southport to keep Maria company while Juan went off to work.

"No, wait, yes, tell her I'm looking forward to seeing her again."

Mack had an international call put through. The telephone rang in Southport, Long Island, and Carol picked up the phone.

"Hello?"

"Hi, this is Mack. Carol? Is Maria all right?"

"Yes, of course, Mack. She is almost completely recovered. She is getting the twins up. I'll get her. Hold on."

Soon enough, Maria picked up the telephone. "Mack! How wonderful to hear your voice. Where are you? Morocco? What are you doing there?"

Mack gave Maria a short-hand account of our recent misadventures, and promised we would be back home in a few days.

Maria said, "Well, don't take too much time getting here, Mack. We have a honeymoon to finish."

After ringing off, Mack strolled out along the terrace of the hotel, looking at the moon over the Bay of Tangier, thinking romantic thoughts about his wonderful, strong wife, a woman who had been through so much, yet had so much strength and patience for her future with a retired school teacher. As he leaned over the stone railing, looking at the disused garden, Mack heard a step behind him. Thinking it was Sal, he started to turn, then felt a sharp needle prick in his arm. Suddenly, oblivion.

Chapter 38

When I got up the next morning, I went to Mack's room and knocked on the door. There was no answer, so I knocked louder. Still no answer. I pushed on the door, and it swung open. Mack was not there, but his suitcase was. I figured he had gone down to breakfast without me. The elevator was not working, had not worked in years, apparently, so it took me a few minutes to descend the dusty stairs. Arriving in the lobby, I looked into the dining room. Mack was not there. I walked over to the main desk, and asked the clerk, "Have you seen my traveling companion? He is not in his room, and not in the dining room."

The clerk smiled, then said, "Ah, you mean Mr. MacIntosh? He came in late last night, accompanied by two men. He looked a little ill, as if he had too much to drink. They were supporting him, as he could barely stand."

"Why didn't you call me?"

"Unfortunately, sir, the phones are not working on your floor. Anyway, one of the men who was helping Mr. Macintosh was familiar to us. It was the man you asked about earlier, Mr. Leroy Kemp. He said your friend was ill, and they were going to take him to the hospital. They asked me to call a taxi and left."

I almost reached across the desk to grab this officious fool when he reached down and picked up an envelope.

He said, "Mr. Kemp asked me to give this to you, Sir."

The note read as follows:

Dear Sal,

The chase is over. I'm tired of playing games with you and Mack. I have a simple proposition for you. You have our money, which our friends in Colombia would like to have as soon as possible. We have your friend. If you want Mack to stay alive, meet me at the Real Club de Campo, the golf course in Malaga, at noon the day after tomorrow. Be there, or be square. Your friend's life depends on it.

—Leroy

Chapter 39

When Mack woke up, he found himself tied hands and feet on the floor of a fishing boat that plowed through the smooth waters of the Mediterranean Sea. Dawn was just breaking in the east, and in the dim light he could see two men. One turned from the helm and grinned wolfishly at Mack's groans. It was Joseph Caddy, who said, "Ah, Leroy, our sleeping beauty is awake."

Mack looked at the other occupant of the boat. It was Leroy Kemp, rubbing the sleep out of his eyes. He said, "Good morning, Mack. I trust you slept well. Sorry if the accommodations are not to your liking, but we had to leave Tangiers in rather a hurry. How do you feel?"

Mack felt as if he had the hangover of all hangovers, even though he had stopped drinking many years ago, but he wasn't going to give his captors any satisfaction. He said,

"You could have picked a better boat, Leroy. This stinkpot smells to high heaven."

Kemp said, "As ever, the joker. Mack, this boat has been used by Joseph and his friends for many errands across the Mediterranean, and on off days, it is used by local fishermen, who are not so neat in their habits, I will admit. But it serves our purpose."

"So, what's the deal, Leroy? Obviously you don't plan to kill me, you haven't dumped me over the side yet."

"No, no, Mack. Give me some credit. Do you think I would stoop so low as to do that?"

"Well, you already have orchestrated several attempts on my life. What's stopping you now?"

"Mack, Mack. Before, you were just an annoying pest, blocking our plans on Long Island and Scotland. Now you are worth something to me."

"What's that?"

Kemp sneered, "Now you are worth one million Euros, the money Sal picked up after Joseph's abortive and unnecessay attack in Scotland. Where is the money, by the way?"

"That might be a problem for you, Leroy. It's in a bank, the Royal Bank of Scotland in Nairn, in the police department account."

Kemp smiled, "Well, we will have to see about making a withdrawal, won't we?"

With those words, he pulled out a hypodermic needle and plunged it into Mack's arm before he realized what he was doing. As he began to black out, Mack thought he saw the lights of the shore ahead.

Later, Mack awoke with a pounding headache, the hangover of all time. He wondered what he had been injected with, hoping it did not have long-term effects. He looked at his new surroundings in the dim light cast from a small, cloudy window. He was in some kind of shed, and from the smell of fertilizer and the clutter of tools, it looked like a greens keeper's base of operations. He was still tied up, but there was a bottle of water and a loaf of bread nearby. Obviously, Leroy wanted him kept alive.

Chapter 40

After getting off the ferry at Algeceris, I rented a car and headed down the coast for Malaga. After a few hours of high speed driving, I pulled into the Real Club de Campo, parked the car, and headed for the clubhouse. Once there, I found Leroy Kemp sitting at the bar, enjoying a cigar and a glass of scotch.

"Hello, there, Sal. I see you made it in good time."

"You bastard, what have you done with Mack?"

"Oh, he's all right. A slight hangover from the narcotic cocktail we gave him, but he seems to be otherwise in good health. Let's see if we can keep it that way, shall we?"

I said, "O.K., let's talk business."

Kemp smiled, then said, "That's what I always liked about you, Sal. No bullshit, just get right to the point. Well, here's the deal. We have Mack. You have our money. Our friends in Colombia were supposed to get that money a month ago, and are getting impatient. On our little sea voyage, I found out from Mack that most of the money is sitting in a bank in Scotland."

At this statement, he pointed to a laptop computer sitting on the bar, and said, "I am going to give you an account number. You will then call Detective Inspector Jamieson in Scotland and tell him to initiate a wire transfer of the money to our account. When the transfer is successful, Joseph and I will go our way, and you will be reunited with Mack. Simple, no?"

It looked like I didn't have any alternative, so I agreed to Kemp's terms. He said, "I thought you would see it my way. The reason in that Jesuit education you had comes through once again, Sal."

He gave me the account number, and I called Jamieson in Scotland. He was expecting my call, and said he would take care of the transfer. After hanging up the phone, I said, "Jamieson said it will take an hour or so. The bank hasn't opened yet."

Kemp smiled expansively, saying, "Well, the important thing is that the deal is going through. Say, why don't we play a round of golf while we are waiting, just for old times' sake?"

I was shocked at the suggestion. How callous could the man be? He had orchestrated murders, made attempts on our lives, kidnapped Mack, and now he wanted to play a round of golf? This was madness. Then the thought occurred to me: maybe it was madness. Maybe after all his travails, Leroy Kemp had finally gone off the deep end, sinking into insanity and despair.

I rallied my wits, and said, "Sure, Leroy. Why not? It might give you a chance to get back some of the money I took from you at the last faculty tournament."

He reddened for a moment, recalling the embarrassment of the tournament he usually won until I came on the scene, then said, "Let's make it interesting, Sal. Think of it this way: we will be playing for Mack's health. If you win, I will make sure he is delivered to you in good condition. If I win, he might be roughed up a little, but still alive. How does that sound?"

"Leroy, you always were a sadistic bastard, but you're on."

We rented some clubs and engaged the services of a couple of antiquarian caddies who looked as if they had fought in the Spanish Civil War.

Built in 1928, the Real Club de Campo is the oldest course on the Spanish mainland. The course turned out to be part links, part parkland, where golfers have to navigate through stands of well-established palm trees and natural lagoons on the Mediterranean coast. It was a flat course, with wide fairways, but the trees could make things difficult. In short, it was just my kind of course. With my bad knees, I wasn't fond of courses where I would have to climb a lot of hills. I have a strong drive, but my short game is spotty. As we teed off on the first hole, the silence was shattered by the sound of a jet airplane landing at the nearby international airport, the one that Mack and I had intended to use in returning to the states. The sound of the plane rattled Kemp, and his drive went wide towards the river and the bird refuge that lay to one side of the course. A flock of cranes and other indigenous birds rose in a clatter of calls as the plane landed. My drive went generally in the same direction, but farther, and as we started off, I said to Kemp,"What happened, Leroy? Where did it start to go wrong for you?"

He said, "When you guys started messing up my operation on the island, that's where."

I answered, "No, I mean before that. You were a pretty good coach, had a nice house, were pulling down what? Over $100,000 a year? That's not chump change, even on Long Island, where the median income was about $55,000."

"Yeah," he said, "We were doing OK, but then, when I retired, I was only making seventy percent of my best five final years. What with property taxes going up, and the cost of living too, a $75,000 pension doesn't go a long way any more."

I said, "I know what you're saying. That's why Mack and I went into business."

He sneered, "Yeah, but you guys are small change. How much could you make extra?"

I said, "We were getting by, making enough to feed our golf habit."

He said, "Well, things were getting tight for me and Mae. You know, she likes to live large, the latest clothes, a new car every year. Then I was approached by Rosario, one of my clamming kids, who had a proposition for me. Seems that he had an 'uncle' in Colombia who wanted to deliver some packages to the Island at night. Wanted to drop them in the water in a safe location, where they could be picked up and delivered to the city. That's where our smuggling operation began. The risk was minimal, the rewards were large."

As we worked our way along the seaside course, he continued, in almost a kind of confessional: "Later, we were doing so well, our friends from Colombia invited me to take a little trip to their central office. That's when they laid the plan to take some of their money and put it into Long Island real estate, which in those days was booming. It was a sure thing, a good way to launder illegal money by buying hot properties like golf courses and condos. That's when you guys came in and put a monkey wrench in the works."

I said, "Yeah, I guess we got lucky. But when you guys started to get rough, we got mad, and even more stubborn in our investigation. It didn't hurt that we had the blessing of the local cops."

As we approached the third green, Kemp said, "After I had to go on the run, things really started to go sour. Mae filed for a divorce, and is still getting half of my pension. The other half has been frozen, with all my other assets, by the feds. I had to leave the country in a hurry, and had nowhere to go but Colombia. My friends down there decided to set me up in Scotland, in the import-export business. They liked single-malt scotch, it turns out, and wanted a reliable, Anglo-looking guy, running their Scottish operation. They never completely trusted Caddy and his gang of gypsies, you know."

After driving off the fourth tee, we strolled along the flat fairway. Kemp continued, "Things were going all right in Scotland until you fellas showed up. I didn't believe it at the time. The two guys I hated most in the world showing up on my doorstep in Scotland."

Later on, he calmed down, and said, "Anyway, I'm over all that now. I don't want anyone hurt. I just want our money back, and be on my way."

After playing nine holes, I was ahead by four strokes. Kemp looked wrung out, by the heat or the emotion of his confession, I couldn't tell. He said, "Let's get a drink and see if the transaction has gone through."

He retrieved his laptop from a locker and joined me at the bar, where I was sipping a refreshing *cerveza*. He turned the laptop on, and after a moment, a smile of satisfaction appeared on his face. "Well, Sal, looks as if your friends in Scotland came through for you. The money has arrived in the designated account."

With those words, he handed me the key to a car, saying, "You will find Mack in the trunk of a Ford Taurus in the back parking lot. Better hurry, I imagine it has been getting hot in there." He smiled maliciously, and slid off the barstool. Picking up the laptop, he headed for the door, adding, "Have a nice trip back to the states, Sal."

I took the key and rushed out to the parking lot. As I looked around, I saw Kemp get into a Land Rover driven by Joseph Caddy. I shrugged my shoulders and started looking for the Taurus. Unfortunately, a Taurus is a popular rental in Andalusia, and there seemed to be many of them in the lot. I ran from car to car, trying the key in the truck lock. On the fifth try, towards the back of the lot near a greens keeper's shed, I found a car where the key worked. As I pulled open the truck lid, I saw Mack, still tied up, shaking his head and rolling his eyes wildly. He was trying to tell me something. Suddenly I heard a ticking noise, getting louder and louder. I grabbed Mack in my arms, and dove for a ditch at the side of the parking lot. As we hit the muddy water, there was a loud explosion, and a sheet of flame shot over our heads. The car had been booby-trapped. So much for the confession and good will of one Leroy Kemp.

Chapter 41

I untied Mack, who seemed to be unhurt, and we climbed out of the muddy ditch, as golfers rushed up to look at the flaming car. We were picked up in a jeep by my "caddies," who turned out to be undercover members of the Guardia. At the end of the winding road that leads out of the course, we came upon a police roadblock. Kemp and Caddy stood to one side in handcuffs, surrounded by Spanish police and Interpol agents. As we got out of the jeep and approached them, Caddy started cursing in several languages. I didn't know Kurdish, but I could pick out a few choice Spanish phrases, such as "Hijo de puta." Oh well, sticks and stones. Kemp sneered, "Well, you survived again, Mack. But at least we got our money back."

A Spanish police officer said, "But you will not enjoy it,

Señor, for you will be spending time in our jail for kidnapping and attempted murder."

Kemp said, "I'm sure our lawyers will have us out in no time. Meanwhile, the money has gone to South America, where it belongs."

An Interpol agent spoke up, saying, "I would not be too sure of that, my friend. Soon after Mr. Cascio arrived in Spain, he called authorities in Scotland and they set up what is called a 'blind transfer'."

I said, "Yeah, when I called Don in Scotland, he contacted Interpol, and their computer guys set it up so it would look as if the money had gone through to your account. Don sure wasn't going to let any of the money we had set aside for his widows and orphans fund to get out of Scotland, you know."

Mack added, "If and when you guys get out of jail, I would not head back to Colombia, if I were you."

Chapter 42

That night we checked into the *parador* on a hill overlooking the bullring in Malaga. After a refreshing shower and change of clothes, we went to dinner in the parador's restaurant, and watched the lights go on in the cruise ships as they docked in the harbor. Taking a taste of wine for the first time in many years, Mack said, "I could get used to this kind of living."

"Me, too," I answered. "But we have better things to do with our new-found wealth. Don't forget, half of it stays in Scotland for your 'cousin's' various projects."

Mack said, "Yeah, you're right. And there are many worthwhile causes at home to which we can contribute. I always wanted to give more money to the Cancer Society and other causes, but just couldn't afford to. Now we can."

I said, "Before we get carried away with our new

munificence, let's talk to Maria and Carol, and maybe blow some of the money on a nice trip to the Mohonk Mountain House in New Paltz. I'll bet they would like a week or so up there."

"Works for me. They have a nice little nine-hole golf course up there, too. Did you know that?"

Epilogue

Dear Joe,

I thought I would write to you and tell you about our Scottish adventure. As you can see from the attached pages, we played a lot of golf, and stirred up an equal amount of trouble.

As for the Scottish oil industry, things seem to be back on an even keel, and the Scots are making money hand over fist.

You might be interested to know that Laird Gump's golf project has gone belly up. A lot of people in that neighborhood, folks who were sympathetic to the Mcleans and their relatives, still suspect Gump of foul play, and do not take kindly to ugly Americans who try to throw their money around. The course opened with all sorts of fanfare, naturally, but Gump ran into a number of obstacles. Permits were denied by local authorities, the restaurant was found to have many unsanitary practices, and the unkindest cut of all, nobody wanted to work for the Laird as a caddy. Golf carts are not permitted, of course, and rich golfers do not like to carry their bags.

We are all back in the states now after a side trip to Spain by way of France and Morocco. We got lucky again, and were able to get out of the trap that Leroy Kemp and his sidekick set for us.

Mack and I are back at the old shop, going after disability cheaters and insurance scams. Our latest case involves a couple of retired ball players who have set up something called the 9/11 Firefighters Foundation. They sponsor golf tournaments and the like, trading on their dubious fame as ballplayers and public sentiment regarding 9/11, raising money to give to firefighters' families. The thing is, they keep about 70 percent for "administrative" costs and dole out relatively small amounts to needy families and fire departments. We tracked the outfit down to their "office," a kitchen in someone's home in Farmingdale.

Juan is back on the job in the city, and doing better than ever. The *abuelitas* in his neighborhood were glad to see him, and even more excited to find that he is going to get married as soon as his girl friend, Mary Soames from Scotland, finishes the nursing program at Adelphi University. Seems that she got a scholarship from an outfit called the Cascio Foundation.

Well, that's about all the news, old buddy.

Give us a call next time you're in the area. I would be glad to take your money again.

Your friend,

Sal

also available from publishamerica
IN THE NAME OF CHURCH
By Edmund DuBois

In 1572, there is an uneasy peace in the bitter religious wars between Catholics and Protestants in France. Madeleine, daughter of a nobleman, and Colette, her bright but unlettered maid, find themselves fending off strange attempts by a Catholic bishop who is determined to take control of the maid because he professes to believe she is bewitched. A royal wedding in Paris provides the opportunity for Madeleine to seek excitement and shield Colette from the bishop. Madeleine and Colette have romantic affairs, but the Saint Bartholomew's Day massacre of Protestants turns the happy royal marriage into macabre tragedy and gives the bishop the chance to attempt his evil intentions- yet once again, Colette escapes. In a final confrontation, the bishop's true motive is unmasked, and believing himself possessed by the Devil, he goes insane. Madeleine, because of the terrible happenings "In the name of church," disavows affiliation with any church, and takes her worship directly to God.

Paperback, 531 pages
6" x 9"
ISBN 1-4137-1763-2

About the author:

Edmund DuBois is a retired Army officer. He served in the Pacific during World War II and subsequently had assignments in the Pentagon and with NATO. He has co-authored one publication and is working on a sequel to the present novel. He resides in Sonoma, California.

available to all bookstores nationwide.
www.publishamerica.com